Her first thought was that they had sunk…

Then the deck heaved upward against her, and she clung to Alex as the spray crashed over *Mistral*'s decks.

They were at the top of an unbelievably long valley of seawater, a dizzying green slope that yawned open like some vision of Hell in a medieval painting. And now they were racing down it with ghastly speed, heading for the maelstrom at the bottom.

As they hurtled into the abyss, Nicolette buried her mouth against Alex's hard shoulder, watching with terrified eyes as the mountain of water, impossibly vast, gathered above them. She squeezed her eyes shut, grateful in some tiny corner of her soul that she was at least with Alex, that they were going to be buried under that terrible mass of water together….

Books by Madeleine Ker

HARLEQUIN ROMANCES
2595—VOYAGE OF THE MISTRAL

HARLEQUIN PRESENTS
642—AQUAMARINE
656—VIRTUOUS LADY

These books may be available at your local bookseller.

For a free catalog listing all titles currently available,
send your name and address to:

Harlequin Reader Service
P.O. Box 52040, Phoenix, AZ 85072-9988
Canadian address: Stratford, Ontario N5A 6W2

Voyage of the Mistral

Madeleine Ker

Harlequin Books

TORONTO • NEW YORK • LONDON
AMSTERDAM • PARIS • SYDNEY • HAMBURG
STOCKHOLM • ATHENS • TOKYO • MILAN

Original hardcover edition published in 1983
by Mills & Boon Limited

ISBN 0-373-02595-5

Harlequin Romance first edition January 1984

CHAPTER ONE

THE thunder had been muttering in the hills all afternoon, but Nicolette had gazed up into the blue African sky before setting out, and had decided that the storm was miles away yet.

But it wasn't.

The ominous thunderclouds, heaped up like vast bales of dirty wool in the sky, had gathered with incredible swiftness over the violet hills of Serengeti. And the thunder was no longer a distant mutter, but had become a harsh boom that was beginning to frighten Nicolette. Somewhere ahead, the sky leaked a vivid dribble of lightning, and the angry response rolled around the iron hills and across the dry yellow bush. She shivered, and twisted the key futilely in the Ford's dashboard. The starter-motor whined feebly, and choked into silence. Breathing a prayer, she tried again. And again. The middle of an extensive game reserve—which counted lions and hyenas amongst its denizens—was not the best place for a breakdown.

Twisting the key now only produced a few plaintive clicks. The battery was obviously exhausted. Nicolette thumped the steering wheel in frustration. What awful, what awfully *typical* bad luck! Some jinx was on her lately, that was for sure. She peered around the dense, khaki-coloured bush, a sea of dry grass dotted here and there with thorn trees and acacias, as if expecting to meet a

lion's tawny eyes. What the devil was she going to do?
There was little humour in being stuck on a dirt track in
the middle of Serengeti, ten miles from camp, with a
non-functioning car, and a rapidly-brewing thunderstorm. She must have been mad to set out on her own that
afternoon. She had left the five others behind, playing
cards in the rest camp, because she was unwilling to waste
her last day in the game reserve. To-morrow they were
driving back to Mombasa, back to the *Elsie*, Julian's big
motor-launch, to sail back to Britain. She looked up at the
sky. It had not escaped her attention that the time-space
between the lightning and the thunder was growing
steadily shorter. The storm was coming her way. Could
she make it back to the camp before it broke? She twisted
in her seat to stare at the road behind her. Nothing. No
comforting shape of another car on the little dirt track. No
grey shapes of wildebeest. Nothing but the rolling savannah. And what was more, Nicolette realised bitterly,
nobody was likely to be setting off in this weather, either.
There was going to be no traffic on the roads this afternoon. In fact, nobody but a mad fool would have left camp
anyway.

'Damn!' she muttered.

She recalled the game warden's strict warning never to
set foot outside the car in the confines of the reserve.
'Serengeti is not a zoo,' he had told them, his pale blue
eyes grim. 'The bush is filled with animals which can—
and do—attack humans. Never get out of your car, no
matter what the reason.'

'And if you break down?' someone had asked.

'Then you wind up your windows and *sit tight*,' he had
replied. 'Help will arrive sooner or later—we patrol all the

roads in the reserve regularly, so you'll have nothing to worry about. But if you get out of your car, and try to make it on foot, all they're likely to find of you will be a few chewed bones.' At the time, Nicolette had made appropriate noises of horror. But now, as she sweltered in her car, the elderly game warden's injunction was beginning to sound rather theatrical. After all, she had not seen a single animal on her drive this afternoon.

Admittedly, her thoughts had been on Mark, as usual. And other gloomy topics. So she was probably not paying very much attention anyway. But apart from a few birds and the odd lizard, the bush had seemed as empty as though she were the last living creature on the dusty face of the earth. The thunder rumbled hugely, and she wiped sweat from her upper lip.

How regularly did they patrol the roads? Once a day? Once a year? Nicolette sighed in frustration. The idea of an African holiday (Kenya welcomes you with its fabulous game reserves, its beautiful beaches) had seemed such a perfect escape from her heartache over Mark Macmillan. And his uncertainties and doubts that were making her life a misery. She had envisaged palm-trees and long cool drinks, somewhere comfortable, where you could sit and watch the animals grazing, and listen to the tom-toms or whatever. Not *this*—this arid landscape overshadowed by thunderclouds and unbearably hot, and certainly not being stuck in a hired car, miles from any damned where, with no prospect of rescue, no water, and no—she rummaged in the glove compartment—no liquorice allsorts! She wiped her forehead, and surveyed the savannah with troubled brown eyes.

The thought of baking here like a lobster for two or

three days—or starving to death, or being struck by lightning within the next few minutes, was beginning to make the prospect of meeting something wild and hungry in the bush seem almost attractive. Ten miles was a long walk; but the route was simple enough. And she was a fit young woman of twenty-three. Well, twenty-two and three quarters. And being drenched in the rain would at least be an improvement on the intolerable muggy heat that was building up in the car. Besides, no one would even know where to look for her.

Her mind made up, Nicolette swung her long legs out of the car, locked the doors, and began to trudge along the red dirt road towards the rest camp. It was cooler in the open air. Just. She looked back at the blue Ford, feeling that she had made the right decision. She smiled, a gentle smile that transformed a pretty face into a lovely one, and stretched her arms out. Imagine sitting in that car for a day! The picture of a skeleton sitting patiently behind the wheel crossed her mind. What an ironic end that would have been for twentieth-century woman, starving to death, trapped in her little technological cage, too timid to step out into the big, bad world. It was an amusing thought. And after all, there was considerable glamour in a ten-mile hike through a lion-ridden game reserve. She would tell the story quite casually, of course. She could see the grizzled game warden's eyes widening with amazement and admiration as she coolly told him that his precious reserve was not nearly as dangerous as he liked to think!

But when the red dirt road took her around a little hill, and the blue Ford disappeared from sight, and she found herself utterly alone in an unhospitable African landscape, her heart unaccountably sank. The journey ahead suddenly seemed an extremely long and possibly unpleasant one. Ten miles! And all those lions! She had watched them basking in the sun by the shores of the big lake. They had looked like big house-cats. Very big house-cats. She stopped and looked back, ready to run as fast as she could back to her little technological cage, with its lockable doors, its rainproof roof, and its comfortable vinyl seats. The thunder rumbled again. She shook the cowardly thought away, and strode on bravely.

Her mind soon returned to the subject which never seemed far away—Mark Macmillan. Handsome, clever Mark, with his slow smile. Rich Mark, who could never quite make his mind up whether their engagement was on or off. 'It's not that I don't care for you, Nicky,' he had said, patting her cheek. 'I do. It's just that—well, I'm not sure of myself. I'm not sure of anything any more. You go and enjoy your safari, and I'll think things over here in London. We'll talk about it when you get back. Okay?'

Dumbly, she had nodded, trying not to show him how miserable she felt inside. Mark might not be sure about *her*, but she was certainly sure about Mark. She had never met anyone like him before, clever, sophisticated, successful. Everything he touched seemed to turn to gold. They shared a common interest in painting and music—that was how they had met in the first place. He was so right for her.

And what was more, she was forced to admit, Mark's kisses had introduced her to a new world of experience. She had been so innocent before she met him, knowing so little about herself or the world. That night—when they had lain together on the couch, and she had allowed his hands and lips to explore her body for the first time—still haunted her. He had aroused feelings in her, confusing, delicious feelings, which she never knew could exist. She had discovered a hunger, a puzzling, quickening desire that was new to her. And Mark was responsible for it. She had stopped him, somewhat to his disgust, long before anything serious could happen. But she had realised that there was a limit, and beyond that limit she would lose her self-control, sliding with pounding heart and fluttering stomach over the waterfall of passion.

She glanced absently around the flat hills and the thorn trees, lost to the world around her. Mark seemed to know so much about—that sort of thing. She had wondered where he had acquired that knowledge, and then had bitten the jealous thought back. That was all in the past now. Because he loved her, and she—did she love him? Of course she did. And when they had discussed getting engaged, Mark had been eager, holding her hand and looking deep into her brown eyes. In the absence of her parents—she was so sure they would have loved Mark—there was no one to impede the arrangement.

Mark's parents, of course, had rather looked down on her. In the nicest possible way. Mrs Macmillan was actually the Honourable Cynthia, and Mr Macmillan was Lord Someone's son. Or was he Sir Something Someone's son? Anyway, a prospective daughter-in-law who was *in trade* (art restoring) had not thrilled them to bits. But she had felt she was winning them slowly round. Until things had begun to go wrong with Mark. He had begun to look at her with doubt in his blue eyes, to sigh with boredom in her company, to want to make love to her, and then to get bitter when she said no. To say that he wasn't sure of himself, he wasn't sure of anything any more. For the thousandth time, she wondered what had come between them. Was it something that she had done? Something that—

Nicolette spun round with thumping heart, her thoughts whirling from London to the still heat of the bush. Something had crossed the road behind her—she was sure of that. She stood tensely, straining her ears for a repetition of the sound. Paws or hooves? It was probably some small antelope, she told herself. The overcast sky rumbled distantly, then louder. The silence that followed was eerie. The bush was waiting. Even the incessant shrilling of the cicadas had stopped. Nicolette walked onwards, feeling very small against the vastness of the bush. She had chosen to wear cowboy boots, beautifully-tooled things that she had bought in Mombasa. But the high heels twisted awkwardly in the red sand. She brushed the sweat off her upper lip again, wondering absently whether her smell was carrying on the tiny breeze. Was some black snout somewhere sniffing curiously at this strange smell, composed of hot human, assorted textiles, leather, sweat, and Diorissimo?

The landscape brooded around her. She tried to think of Mark again. And so. So, they had agreed to part for three weeks. She was going to take her leave in Africa, and he was going to work through the silly season at home. What would be waiting for her when she got back? A loving reconciliation? I'm sorry, darling, but I can't go through with it? And was there, she wondered unhappily, a strain of cynicism creeping into the way she thought about Mark?

What was that noise? Surely nothing could hear her heels in the soft sand? Everything would be sheltering under a tree now, waiting for the coming storm. The bush jacket she wore was beginning to stain black under the armpits now. How far had she come? Perhaps a mile. Maybe less. She glanced nervously over her shoulder, pulled off the jacket, and slung it wearily over her shoulder. It was going to be good to get back to the sea. She had been going to fly to Kenya at first; but when Mark had discovered that Julian Mitchell, one of his friends, was planning a cruise from London to Mombasa in *Elsie*, a sleek motor-launch, he had insisted that it was the ideal opportunity. There was a spare berth on *Elsie*. What was more, Julian and his four friends were even planning to visit Serengeti—she could go with them, couldn't she? Nicolette had not been over-keen at first. She did not entirely trust Julian, and the rich, spoiled set he moved with were not exactly her cup of tea. Besides, she had protested, the long cruise would cut into her time at Serengeti. But Mark had been insistent. And, as usual, she had done what Mark wanted.

The cruise from Britain had been pleasant enough. Having discovered that Nicolette was not quite their 'sort', the five young people had left her more or less to do as she pleased. She had basked in the sun, or read countless romances, watching with one eye as the others enjoyed themselves in their own way—the jokes that only they could understand, references to people called 'Jumbo' or 'Topsy', a lot of hard drinking and upper-class horse-play. She had been determined not to look a gift horse in the mouth. But she had wondered what her father would have said about the five companions of her voyage—the Famous Five, she had privately christened them.

Despite the darkening sky, the road ahead shimmered in a heat haze. She was very hot. Again, she cast a quick glance over her shoulder. It was difficult to shake off the eerie feeling that she was being watched. Maybe she should have stuck it out in the car? Would the Famous Five have had the brains to send out a search party for her, when she failed to return? She glanced at her watch. By now they were probably on their third or fourth Piña Coladas and dry Martinis, and would be laughing hysterically at their own in-jokes. She grimaced to herself. It had taken this holiday to show her just what twits Mark's friends could be. She glanced back. Her T-shirt was wet, and clung to her uncomfortably. When she got back to the camp, she promised herself, she was going to take a long, hot bath, and a long, cool drink. And then she was going to order a thick, juicy—

Another slight sound made her spin round in panic. There *was* something there. Something following her through the long grass. She stood rooted to the spot, her ears straining for any noise. Suddenly, a frightful image came into her mind, filling her with terror. The hyenas! She thought of their huge, ugly heads, the massive jaws that could crush bones like so much dry toast, the teeth that could rend and rip. She had learned at Serengeti that hyenas were not, as popular opinion believed, merely scavengers. They were hunters, the most ruthless, cruel, relentless hunters in Africa, with their hideous, loping walk, their lowering black heads, their eyes of fire.

'Oh, dear God!' she breathed shakily, her oval face white with tension. She listened.

The lightning was like a sheet of white fire, and the thunder ripped overhead, a noise as shockingly violent as if giant hands had torn the sky in half. Nicolette started in alarm, and looked up anxiously. The first heavy drops of rain had begun to fall, splashing into the sand like blood. The road ahead to the camp stretched interminably into the empty, sinister landscape. What had led her to imagine that Africa was all jungle and waving banana trees? This vast grey sky was as pitiless as a desert, the grass dry and juiceless. Even the red earth seemed parched, drinking up the large raindrops as they fell. Too afraid to look back again, she walked through the ever-increasing rain. Soon she was soaked, her long blonde hair straggling uncomfortably across her cheeks, dripping water down the back of her neck.

Another vast crash of thunder shook the universe. This was not like English thunder; this was savage, primaeval, a terrible violence huge enough to smash worlds. The thunder rolled from one corner of the horizon to the other, and then over her head, like boulders rolled on heaven's roof. Again there came that sound behind her, this time loud enough to rise above the pelting of the rain. It was a distinct rustle in the grass. She whipped around, catching the tall fronds swaying. Was it the rain, or—a grunt emerged from the grass, and Nicolette ran.

Her heart pounding in her throat, her breath rasping painfully, she slipped in the red mud, rose, slipped again. The beating rain was reducing the track to a quagmire, and her elegant cowboy boots slithered helplessly. She looked back, and her blood froze. Two dark shapes were materialising behind her on the road. Hyenas! She crouched, petrified, in the shelter of the long grass. If she lay still, would they miss her? No. They would catch her smell, the frightened human smell that would tell them food was near. The thought filled her heart with sick terror. She leaped to her feet, and ran on blindly through the mud, looking desperately for a tree, anything to hide in. Without knowing it, she was gasping out Mark's name, 'Mark—please help me—'

She cast a wild glance over her shoulder. They were following her! The two grim black shapes, heads down to the earth, were drawing steadily closer. Despair tore at her. Too exhausted to go further, she stumbled to her knees, her heart pounding as though it would burst, her throat dry with fear. Then two brilliant lights flashed through the lashing rain ahead of her, and a big white shape began to materialise. Her heart almost stopped—then bounded with a surge of joy. It was a car, a Range Rover with tinted windows, lurching and slithering through the mud towards her. With a final spurt of energy, she struggled to her feet and waved frantically. Another crash of thunder battered at her eardrums as the big vehicle stopped, and a tall man in boots and a grey flak-jacket jumped out.

She stumbled forward and threw herself into his arms, pressing her face against his broad chest, and gabbling confused thanks as strong arms encircled her. Then her knees gave way, and she sagged against him, so that he was forced to pick her up bodily and heave her on to the front seat. A trembling reaction set in as she shut her eyes, hoping she wasn't going to be sick. Then she opened them.

'Welcome aboard,' said a big, tanned man with a beard.

'Thank God you came,' she gasped, gazing into a pair of

calm, smoky grey eyes. 'You saved my life! There were hyenas chasing me, two of them—'

'Hyenas?' The deep voice was incredulous. Nicolette followed his gaze. Standing forlornly in the rain a few dozen yards away were two young warthogs, their naturally mournful faces made ridiculous by mud and rain. As she gaped at them, they turned with military precision, and with their stubby tails held high, trotted off into the bush.

'Oh,' she said.

'Don't sound so disappointed,' he said drily. 'They might just as easily have been hyenas.' He walked round the car, and climbed into the driver's seat. 'What were you doing out of your car anyway?'

She looked up into the bearded face with a timid smile.

'It broke down,' she explained, 'so I decided to walk back to camp—'

'In a thunderstorm? Alone and unarmed?' Black eyebrows rose gently.

'Well,' she said defensively, 'I didn't know whether anyone would ever come to my rescue out there. Thank God you came, anyhow.' The beautiful eyes were watching her with uncomfortable clarity. 'It's only ten miles,' she stammered on, 'and I didn't think the storm would break so soon—'

'You don't have to defend yourself,' he said softly. 'If you want to kill yourself, that's your business.' He looked her up and down calmly. 'You've certainly got yourself into a mess, young lady.' Suddenly she realised that her bush jacket was missing.

'Oh,' she said in dismay, 'my jacket! I've dropped it somewhere on the road!'

'When you were being chased by the hyenas?' he suggested with dry irony. She flushed.

'It's got all my money in it—and the car keys—'

He held up a strong brown hand. 'Okay, I've got the message. We'll take a look.' The car started at his touch, and they lurched along the slippery, blood-red road, Nicolette peering out of the windscreen, feeling slightly disturbed by this calm male presence beside her.

'Thank you for finding me, by the way,' she said, 'I don't know what I would have done if you hadn't arrived.'

'Not at all. It's not every day that one gets hugged and kissed by a beautiful stranger.' She shot a quick glance at him, but his face—what she could see of it—was impassive.

'Had you been looking long?' she asked.

'I wasn't looking at all,' he said gently. 'I was actually on my way to meet a friend.'

'Oh,' she said again. His manner was deceptively gentle. The thick beard gave him an almost savage look, and in his supple boots and grey combat gear, he might have been a soldier or a lumberjack. But his voice was quiet and authoritative, and the hands on the steering wheel, though powerful and obviously used to hard work, were not coarse. The grey eyes met hers again, with that hint of mockery in them. They were disconcerting eyes, she decided, their apparent calm concealing a hard challenge.

'I hope you're keeping a look-out for your precious jacket,' he said, and she looked away, flushing.

'There it is,' she said. He stopped, and muttering her thanks, Nicolette scrambled out and went to retrieve it. The cowboy boots slipped uncontrollably in the wet, and with a gasp, she found herself sitting painfully in the middle of a miniature lake. Coated with red slime, she struggled to her feet, casting a hasty glance back at the car. The tinted windscreen concealed the driver's expression. Which was just as well, she reflected with burning cheeks, as she scooped up her jacket, checked that the keys were still in it, and walked back, nursing a bruised arm.

As she opened the door, cool grey eyes met hers wearily.

'Do you have any idea what a state you're in?' he asked quietly. She glanced down at her sodden jeans, at the mud that clung to everything, at the filthy jacket in her arms. She brushed the wet blonde hair out of her eyes, and looked at him.

'I don't make a habit of this,' she sighed.

'I'm glad to hear it,' he said, a glint of humour in his eyes. 'Would you mind riding in the back?'

'I'm sorry?'

'This isn't my car,' he told her expressionlessly. But she had a shrewd idea he was laughing at her. 'I don't want you to ruin the seats, Miss—er—'

'Mercury. Nicolette Mercury.'

'Miss Mercury. I'm sure you'll find somewhere to sit in the back. Perhaps on the spare wheel?'

Miserably she clambered into the back, and wedged herself between a box of tools and the spare wheel, feeling exactly like a muddy dog exiled by indignant owners. 'What about my car?' she ventured.

'I presume it's hired? Then you'd better leave it where it is, and contact the company from the camp.'

'Oh. You really did save my life, you know. If the hyenas hadn't found me, I'd probably have been struck by lightning.'

'Okay. We'll say you owe me a favour.' He met her eyes

in the rearview mirror. 'Tell me, who is Mark?'

'I beg your pardon?' she stammered.

'When you threw yourself into my arms you were babbling about Mark.'

'Yes,' she said, embarrassed, 'I suppose I was. He's—er—he's my fiancé.' Almost, she added to herself.

'Ah. I thought he might have been your patron saint.' She sneaked a sidelong glance at him through the space between the front seats. A big man, broad-shouldered and flat-stomached. The eyes that were watching the road carefully were a flat, challenging grey. Battleship grey. The keen eyes of a hunter, or a sailor. His nose was straight, a strong, arrogant, Norman nose, and the cheekbones were firm. But the lower half of his face was concealed by the thick black beard that was, she now noticed, flecked with gold.

'I thought you were a game ranger at first,' she said. He did not respond. She tried again.

'You aren't a game ranger, are you?'

'What? Oh—no, I'm on holiday.'

'Are you staying in Serengeti much longer?'

'No. I'm leaving to-night.'

'Oh,' she said, obscurely disappointed. 'We're leaving to-morrow.'

'You were very silly to go out on your own in this weather.' He glanced at her in the mirror. 'Won't Mark be angry with you?'

'Well no, actually. Mark's in England.' One eyebrow rose sceptically. 'I came to Serengeti with some friends,' she told him.

'Ah. A last spinster fling before the chains of matrimony?'

'Not exactly. We decided to have—' She stopped herself. She didn't owe this stranger any explanations about her private life. 'Our holidays didn't coincide, that's all,' she concluded. The man's eyes were still watching her in the rearview mirror. Then he shrugged, as if to say it was none of his business anyhow, and the high wooden gateway of Bubi camp loomed out of the rain ahead of them, flanked by its two famous elephant tusks. Nicolette directed him to the hut she was sharing with Julian and his friends. *Hut* being a polite understatement for the palatial bungalow that was the most expensive and luxurious accommodation Serengeti could offer. As he helped her out of the Range Rover, the two girls, Samantha and Geraldine, emerged from the doorway.

'Nicky darling,' cooed Samantha, her gold bangles clinking musically against the glass she was carrying. 'You poor dear! What on earth happened to you?'

'The car broke down,' she said, acutely conscious of her filthy state next to the impeccable elegance of the two women, who were staring from her to her rescuer with curious eyes. 'This gentleman found me.'

'That was very kind of him,' purred Geraldine, her sultry almond eyes flicking over his tall, supple figure. She extended a slim, bejewelled hand. 'My name's Geraldine Parker,' she said. He shook her hand briefly, without speaking, his cool grey eyes taking them in, the glasses in their hands, the pricy 'bush' clothes that were actually made of suede and silk, the abundance of gold and diamonds. Nicolette could tell exactly what he was thinking—rich bitches. Their drawling accents and spoiled faces proclaimed them for what they were. Julian Mitchell strolled out in his turn, also holding a glass, his handsome, slightly petulant face puffy with the brandy he had already drunk.

'Nicky, old thing,' he said, removing the long yellow cheroot from his lips to stare at her muddy clothes. 'What happened? Where's the car?'

'It broke down,' Samantha explained, giving the tall man the benefit of her most winning smile, 'and this kind gentleman gave her a lift back.'

'That was good of you,' drawled Julian, staring at him. 'My name's Julian Mitchell.'

'Alexander St Cloud,' said the bearded man, taking Julian's hand in an unwilling handshake. Julian's eyebrows rose.

'Any relation to Amory St Cloud?'

'I'm afraid not.'

'Well, my dear chap, come on in and have a drink—'

'Please don't bother,' Alexander St Cloud interrupted calmly. There was an ironic glint as he surveyed them all. 'I'm in rather a hurry. I have to meet someone in a few minutes.'

'Please don't go yet,' murmured Geraldine, fluttering her eyelashes. 'Just a *tiny* little drink? Please?'

'Yes, come on, old man,' pressed Julian. 'Just a quick whisky. After all, the sun's over the yard-arm, and—' He stopped, then pointed a triumphant finger at Alexander St Cloud. 'I've got you,' he said. 'You're Paul St Cloud's son, aren't you?'

He nodded, glancing at his watch. 'That's right. Do you know my father?'

'Why, he built my boat,' said Julian, turning to the rest of them. 'And Paul St Cloud's the best boat designer in the business. I'm delighted to see you again, my dear chap. Now look, you must have a drinkie—'

'I'm afraid not,' Alexander St Cloud said firmly. 'Besides, shouldn't—er—Nicky be getting into a hot bath?'

Instantly, Geraldine and Samantha clustered around Nicolette with false cries of sympathy. The bearded man eased himself deftly away from them, and climbed lithely back into the Range Rover. With a quick wave he drove off. The two girls ceased their ministrations, and turned to stare after him regretfully.

'Who was that masked man?' Geraldine murmured.

Samantha shook her head. 'Really, Nicky, how did you manage to pick him up? That's the sexiest hunk of—'

'Hey there,' interrupted Julian with a brittle laugh Samantha was his girl-friend. He took her arm possessively. 'Don't be getting any ideas about other men, Sam. You're with me.'

'Of course I am,' she smiled, kissing him. 'So who is he?'

'Well, his father is one of the top boat designers in Britain—St Cloud Construction. They're marine engineers. As for Alex—I've met him once before, in London. Nice chap, if a bit stiff. Funnily enough, I don't think he's in his father's business. I've got an idea he's got something to do with aircraft. Maybe a pilot? Anyway, he seemed to be in an awful rush. Come on, let's go and have another drink.'

Geraldine stared after the white Range Rover.

'You must introduce him properly when we get back to England,' she said in her purring voice. 'He looks like someone I should know, whatever business he's in.'

'He'd eat the likes of you for breakfast, Gerry,' said Samantha with a bright little smile.

'Would he? I'd like to see who eats who, anyway.'

'As a matter of fact,' drawled Julian, 'I don't think Alex St Cloud would have enough to keep you in furs, my dear Gerry. I seem to remember some rumours that his business had gone bust.'

'What a shame,' murmured Geraldine. 'Perhaps that's why he's wearing that beard? I say, Sammy, d'you think he's hiding from his creditors?'

'He didn't look as though the bailiffs were after him,' commented Samantha. 'Anyway, let's get back inside— I'm getting wet.'

They trooped back into the bungalow, talking and laughing, leaving Nicolette standing wearily on the porch. No one, she thought resentfully, was very worried about *her*.

She thought of Alexander St Cloud's level grey eyes. Hard, calm eyes, that said 'damn you' to the world. He certainly didn't look like a man being hunted by bailiffs. When she next saw him, she must thank him properly. She sighed, surveying her own muddy figure. A long hot bath was going to be heaven. She kicked the worst of the mud off her boots, stretched her tired back, and followed the others into the bungalow.

She really must thank him properly. When next she saw him.

CHAPTER TWO

But she did not see Alexander St Cloud again; and two days later they were back in Mombasa. Julian's boat was ready for them at the boatyard, an elegant white shape amongst the assorted craft that bobbed in the murky brown waters of the harbour. *Elsie* looked like what she was, a rich man's expensive toy. Julian treated the powerful boat the way some men treated their cars, as an extension of his male ego. Out to sea, it wasn't so bad, but Nicolette hated the way he powered the boat so recklessly through crowded harbours. Sometimes he could be both arrogant beyond belief and as foolish as a boy.

Elsie had been refuelled and equipped; they had checked themselves through Immigration and Customs with the harbour authority, and now Julian was making some last-minute checks, a glass of brandy close at hand. Nicolette had gone up to the highest part of the boat, the wheelhouse, to gaze out over the harbour and say her own private farewells to Kenya. She was on her way home. To Mark. The thought did not fill her with its usual pleasure. Was she also undecided, uncertain? God forbid! She looked up at the sprawling city that extended in a wide sweep around the harbour, fronted by coconut-palms, glamorous in the blazing sunlight. The harbour swarmed with boats of every kind, but despite the frantic activity, some providence prevented collisions. There seemed to be an unspoken code which ruled all this marine business and commerce. There was no end to the variety of the boats. Arab dhows with their angular sails competed with shabby little canoes and grimy fishing trawlers. The sleek sailboats drifted among them as gracefully as society ladies. Across the harbour, a tug was nudging a rust-streaked cargo vessel into its berth, and a flotilla of little fishing dories was scattering indignantly out of the way.

Elsie herself was on the point of leaving, and Julian had started the big engines that drove the boat. Sitting quietly in the wheelhouse, Nicolette watched the bustle and clamour of the harbour with regret. She didn't want to leave Kenya after all; her time in this beautiful country had been so short. Too short to take in its strange attraction properly. A curse drew her attention to Julian, who was wrestling with the wheel, complaining that the rudder was stiff. She glanced worriedly at the glass of brandy in his free hand. Why did he have to drink so much? Why now, of all times, just as they were about to leave the harbour? He gulped angrily at the liquor, his face more puffy and red than usual, and pulled out the throttle. The engines howled in protest, lifting a turgid heap of water at the stern. Frank Saunders peered into the wheelhouse.

'Having trouble, Julian?'

'I can handle it,' he retorted surlily. Frank shrugged, and returned to his beer. Samantha and Geraldine had already taken up their favourite positions on the upper deck, lying prone in the tiniest of bikinis, coated in a gleaming emulsion of Bergasol and sweat.

Nicolette turned her attention back to the teeming harbour, watching a group of African boys fishing from a little canoe. The big cargo ship had finally docked with a triumphant hoot of its siren, and the fishing dories were drifting back cautiously. A bright swarm of sailing boats was crossing the middle of the harbour.

'Right,' declared Julian, with aggressive good-humour, 'that's that, then. Come on, everybody—wave goodbye to Kenya. England, here we come!' With another gulp at his brandy, Julian gunned the engines, and *Elsie* surged away from the quayside. The boys in the canoe paddled frantically out of the way, and Nicolette looked up in alarm.

'Please be careful, Julian—it's so crowded!'

'I know what I'm doing,' he grinned. His face was covered with a sheen of sweat, and a knot of anxiety formed in Nicolette's stomach. She prayed that they were going to get out to sea without any mishaps—Julian was in a stupid, reckless mood. As if to underline her thoughts, he tossed off the rest of his brandy with a hand that shook slightly, and grinned at her again.

'Go easy,' she sighed. 'You're going so fast—'

'Don't be such a worryguts, old girl. Let Uncle Julian show you how it's done.'

He was steering the boat through a small group of dories, and Nicolette winced as they almost hit the prow of the nearest one. She caught a glimpse of angry African faces as they surged past. Julian laughed, then stopped, and scowled. The entrance to the harbour was crowded with a queue of sailing boats waiting to get out to sea, and he throttled back the launch impatiently. *Elsie* drifted to a halt, rocking with the movement of the sea. He passed his glass to Nicolette for a refill, but she shook her head.

'Wait until we're out of the harbour,' she pleaded. He shot her an angry glance, but said nothing. Geraldine appeared in the doorway, sleek with suntan oil.

'What are we waiting for?' she demanded. Julian ges-

tured scornfully at the crowd of boats ahead. 'Bloody
sailing vessels,' he informed her. 'Look at them—clogging
up the harbour, as usual. It oughtn't to be allowed.' He
glanced at his expensive gold watch. 'I want to be out to
sea by noon, for God's sake!'

Before Nicolette could stop her, Geraldine had poured
him another drink, and was passing him the glass.

'That'll soothe your temper,' she smiled. He tossed
back the contents, and Nicolette's heart sank. Geraldine
stared languidly at the crowd of sails.

'It's a pretty sight,' she murmured.

'What's pretty about it?' he snapped. 'A lot of damn
fools playing with yachts. I wish to hell they'd hurry up,
we're going to be here all day at this rate.' Suddenly the
wind shifted, and for an instant there was a gap in the
thronging sails. Julian grabbed the wheel. 'Right,' he said,
'now's our chance. I'm going through—to hell with the
queue!' He opened the throttle, and *Elsie* surged forward
into the gap.

'Julian,' Nicolette said urgently, 'stop! You're going to
hit someone—'

'Like hell I will,' he snarled. Geraldine grasped his
shoulder, her almond eyes alight with excitement. The
white steel hull cut through the water like a knife—but
already the gap was closing. A lone yachtsman in a red
catamaran managed to turn his boat in time to avoid
them, and Julian twisted the wheel to miss a second boat.
To her horror, Nicolette saw a third boat sailing across
their path, a beautiful grey yacht with a tall black-and-
white sail like a gull's wing. It was right in *Elsie*'s sights.

'*Julian!*' Nicolette covered her face with her hands as he
tried to spin the wheel, curses spilling from his wet lips.

There was an agonising pause. And then a thump that sent them all staggering across the little wheelhouse. Nicolette uncovered her eyes in time to see the beautiful sail swing past their decks. Someone shouted. There was the tinkle of breaking glass. Geraldine reached the throttle and cut the engine off, and in the deathly silence that followed, *Elsie* swung in a wide circle, still scattering sailboats before her. Julian stared back with a haggard expression; the yacht they had hit was heeled over, the long black-and-white sail dipping towards the troubled surface of the water. Along her polished grey hull was a long scar, and someone was in the water, his orange lifejacket showing bright as he swam slowly back to the stricken yacht.

'Reckon he's all right?' Geraldine whispered. With an effort, Julian tried to pull himself together.

'Of course he's all right,' he said shakily, reaching for the throttle. 'Let's get out of here before the harbour police—'

'No!' Nicolette jumped in front of him, white-faced. 'Are you mad, Julian? Someone might have died back there—'

'Oh, rubbish,' interrupted Geraldine harshly. 'Don't talk like a fool—look, the man's climbing back already. And look, the yacht's upright again.'

The tall sail was once more perpendicular. Sailboats had begun to approach *Elsie* from all sides, and they could hear angry shouts.

'I'm getting out,' said Julian nervously, and reached for the throttle. Nicolette clenched her fists, ready to hit out at him.

'Ahoy, *Elsie*! Ahoy there!' A small boat had pulled

alongside, and an indignant middle-aged face peered up at them. 'I saw that—you went straight into him, you damned fool!'

'He was in my way,' snapped Julian, his hand still hovering over the throttle.

'Nonsense! You were going straight for him. Anyway, you'd better get over there and render assistance, young man—one of the crewmen is hurt.'

'Oh no!' protested Geraldine. 'Honestly, Julian, you are an idiot sometimes!' Samantha and the others were crowding into the wheelhouse.

'Best get back to that yacht, Julian,' said Frank quietly. Julian's face was red, but he grasped the throttle unwillingly, started the launch, and steered slowly towards the grey yacht, which was drifting like a wounded bird on the sluggish water.

'I hope you're all going to stand up for me if there's any trouble,' he muttered out of the corner of his mouth. As *Elsie* steered alongside, he composed his features into an expression of jolly good humour.

'Ahoy there!' he called, trying to read the name of the yacht. '*Mistral*, is it? Are you all right?'

A savagely angry face stared up at them, with a straight Norman nose and a thick black beard.

'Lord Almighty!' snarled Alexander St Cloud. 'I might have guessed it would be you bloody fools! Are you drunk, you great oaf?'

'Now take it easy,' said Julian anxiously. 'Is everything all right down there?'

'No, everything is not bloody well all right!' he snapped, his grey eyes furious. 'You've broken my crew member's arm, and he's losing a lot of blood.' For the first time,

Nicolette noticed the man lying huddled in the stern, the red stain on the white planking. Nausea rose inside her, and she heard Frank curse under his breath. Alexander St Cloud looked as though he wanted to murder them all.

'God in heaven! Don't just stand there,' he rasped. 'Help me get him aboard your battleship—he's got to get to a hospital, and fast!'

The Kenyan doctor came out of the ward, pulling his gloves off, and looked at them with no great enthusiasm. Rich foreign children, Nicolette guessed he was thinking. He took in their worried faces with an ironic twist of his mouth.

'Which of you is Mr St Cloud?' he enquired gently.

'He's not here at the moment—he went down to make a phone call,' said Julian. 'But my name's Julian Mitchell, and I'm—'

'Ah yes. You are the man whose boat did all the damage to Mr Franklin's arm.'

'Well,' said Julian, looking flustered, 'that's putting it a bit strong, doctor. I was—'

'How is Mr Franklin?' Nicolette interrupted. The doctor turned to her with tired eyes, then offered a quick smile.

'He's doing very well. The humerus was snapped cleanly. His upper arm, that is. It's a serious injury, and he has lost a pint or so of blood; but there were no complications. It should set perfectly.' He tugged off his other glove as Nicolette heaved a sigh of relief, and looked at her.

'Are you a friend of Mr Franklin's?'

'No,' she stammered. 'I was on board the other boat. The *Elsie*.'

'Ah.' His expression changed. Just then Alexander St Cloud came into the waiting-room, his eyes dark with worry.

'How is he, doctor? I'm Alex St Cloud.'

'Your crewman is doing well,' smiled the doctor, and repeated what he had told Nicolette. 'He should be discharged in a week, maybe less.' As the doctor walked away down the corridor, Alex turned to them with a forbidding expression on his bearded face.

'I hope you're all pleased with yourselves,' he grated.

Samantha stepped forward, smiling coolly.

'Don't take it like that, Alex—'

'Don't call me Alex, damn you!'

She shrugged. 'Mr St Cloud, then. Your crewman will be as good as new in a few weeks. Don't be angry—'

'As good as new?' he repeated bitterly. 'What do you think he is—some kind of home appliance?' He turned to Julian, who was chewing his lip, and for a minute Nicolette thought he was going to strike him. 'As for you, *skipper*,' he said, emphasising the word with biting sarcasm, 'you ought to be tried for drunken driving!'

'Steady on, old man—'

'I smelt the brandy on your breath,' Alex grated. 'God, I wish you amateur sailors would stick to Loch Lomond, and not go around on the high seas, endangering life and limb!'

Nicolette cleared her throat, and tried a timid smile.

'Mr St Cloud,' she said, 'Alex—we're all so very sorry for your friend. And for your yacht.' She was hot with shame for the others. Alex St Cloud's eyes met hers fiercely, as though he were debating whether to lash out at her, too.

'Rich kids,' he said at last, raking them all with a gunmetal-grey glance. 'Stupid rich kids. I'm going to see Pete.' He pushed through them, and into the ward where his friend was lying.

'"Nice chap", I believe you said, Julian?' Samantha's pretty face sneered. 'I thought he was going to hit you for a minute back there.'

'I wouldn't have blamed him if he had!' said someone in a voice close to tears, and Nicolette realised with vague surprise that it was her own voice. They turned to look at her. Samantha's eyes were cool.

'Oh? And why not, Nicolette?'

'Because he's right—rich kids is exactly what you are,' she said quaveringly. 'Irresponsible children. Don't you realise you could have killed that man? You could have killed them both—'

'Come off your high horse,' advised Geraldine gently. 'You were on the boat too, you know.'

'Of course I know—and I'm so ashamed!'

They stared at her for a few seconds, and then Julian slapped his pocket for the box of cheroots he carried.

'There's no point in hanging around here,' he said, puffing out a cloud of thick smoke at the NO SMOKING sign. 'We'd better try and get our rooms back at the hotel for to-night. There's no sense in setting off again until to-morrow.' He squinted at Nicolette through the smoke. 'Come on, Nicky, let's go.'

'I'll join you later,' she said thickly.

He shrugged, and looked at her for an instant. 'You only came along because Mark Macmillan happens to be a good friend, you know. Otherwise you'd never even have been on my boat. Just remember that, Nicky. You've had a jolly nice free holiday on board *Elsie*—don't push your luck.' He stared into her eyes for a second, then smiled his wide, false grin. 'Okay, Nicky? Right. We'll see you later, at the hotel. Come on, let's get a drink.'

She watched them stroll out with the inborn arrogance of their kind, trying to fight back the tears of mortification, and then sat down on the couch. A large African woman opposite was staring at her curiously. Nicolette closed her eyes and leaned back, remembering the horrible thump as *Elsie*'s sharp prow had hit the grey yacht's elegant hull. There would be expensive repairs to be made, she was certain. And she had been right—they could so very easily have killed the two men on board *Mistral*. What would her father have said? Her father, so big and strong and bear-like, who had taught her to sail before she was ten, who had been so fierce on the subject of safety at sea! She recalled the grizzled face, the powerful arms that could toss a little girl miles into the air, and catch her, shrieking with delight, with the sureness of a trapeze artist. And then one day he had sailed away into the Channel on a foggy morning, and she had never seen him again.

They had found the little sloop, wrecked on the jagged needles of the Minquiers. And that was all. His death had left her utterly alone—except for the grave of the mother she had never known. She was not likely to forget that death was always present at sea. As for Julian and the others—suffering and pain formed no part of their lives. They didn't understand. Their pleasure was all that mattered to them, no matter who got hurt in the process. She opened her eyes as the door opened, and Alex St Cloud came into the room, his face set and bitter.

She stood up nervously, and walked over to meet him.

'What the devil are you doing here?' he growled.

'I—I meant what I said. About being sorry for what we'd done.' She twisted her hands, unable to meet the fierce grey eyes. 'I know it was unforgivable—what Julian did. But they're just kids. You were right about that. They don't know any better, and—and—'

'And so they've sent you to negotiate, eh?'

'No,' she said, meeting his eyes. 'I just wanted to try and explain to you. They're stupid, irresponsible—but they'll grow up one day. And I wanted to say sorry on my own account. I was in that wheelhouse, and I should have stopped Julian. I couldn't. And I'm very sorry . . .'

'Yeah.' His eyes were cold. 'Well, you'd better run along back to them now. You are their little toy doggie, aren't you?'

'What do you mean?' she asked quietly, her face reddening.

He sneered, 'You're the poor relation, aren't you? I can see you're not their type. So they keep you around to do all their dirty work, don't they—like apologising to the poor bloody fools they run over!'

'You're wrong, Mr St Cloud.' She met his eyes without flinching, bitterly hurt. 'I'm not their type, no. And I did come along because Julian is a friend of Mark's. But I'm nobody's little toy doggie.'

He contemplated her for a second, then shrugged.

'Well, run along, then, whatever you are. You make me sick!'

Nicolette turned away, aching. His anger was understandable, and there was nothing she could do to allay it. And was there a grain of truth in what he had said? Was she becoming the poor relation in the rich set that included Mark Macmillan? She turned back to Alex.

'Before I go—is your friend conscious?'

'Just,' he said coldly. 'Why?'

'I'd like to speak to him.'

'To hell with that!'

'I've got a feeling Mr Franklin won't be quite as unforgiving as you are,' she said quietly. She walked past him into the ward. In the far corner, a man was lying back on a pillow, his face pale and tired. A bandage covered his chest, and the arm that lay above the blanket was strapped into a complicated aluminium frame. Nicolette bit her lip. If only the others could be made to see this—the result of their stupidity.

She bent over the white face, and the hollow eyes flickered open.

'Mr Franklin?' she said quietly. 'My name's Nicky Mercury. I was on the *Elsie*—the boat that hit your yacht.' He nodded slightly, eyes misty with drugs and pain. 'I want to tell you how very sorry I am,' she said. 'It was unforgivable of us. I'm sorry, from the bottom of my heart.'

The blue eyes searched hers tiredly, and then he smiled faintly. His good hand fluttered open, and she took it gently in both her own.

'I'll be okay,' he whispered. 'Good doctors. Good nurses. I'll be fine—don't worry.' He smiled again, and the drawn features blurred into the relaxation of sleep. Nicolette laid his hand gently on the coverlet, and stood up. Alex was standing next to her, watching her with grim eyes.

'He won't be sailing for the next year,' he said curtly.

His eyes flicked to the metal frame on his friend's arm, met hers coldly, and then he turned on his heel and walked out.

Nicolette followed slowly. He was waiting for her in the room outside.

'Listen,' he said, 'you tell Mitchell that he's liable for all the expenses on *Mistral*. And it's going to cost him a pretty penny—she's scarcely been built. As for Pete, I'll meet the costs myself. I don't want that dog to pay for his hospital treatment. And tell him that if he wants to argue, he'd better get himself a good lawyer. A very good lawyer.' He turned and walked off.

'Tell him yourself,' Nicolette said quietly.

He stopped, and turned back with furious eyes.

'What did you say?'

'Tell him yourself,' she repeated. 'I'm not carrying your messages around.'

They faced one another angrily. The large African woman stared from one to the other with perplexed eyes.

'Very well,' Alex St Cloud said at last, his voice dry with anger, 'I will tell him myself. Where is he?'

'He'll be at the Mombasa Hilton,' she said. His eyes met hers coldly for a last second, and then he turned and was gone.

'But it wasn't Julian's fault,' said Geraldine plaintively. 'He was going exactly where—'

'Please stay out of this,' Alex said icily. 'You were steering straight at me, Mitchell. I never had a chance to get out of the way. It's going to cost a lot of money to repair *Mistral*—and you're going to be paying.'

'I say,' said Julian Mitchell angrily, 'that's going a bit

far! After all, it's not as if it's structural damage—it's just a few planks smashed. And the surfacing.'

'The surfacing?' Alex repeated bitterly. 'That surfacing is pure liquid nylon, Mitchell. It has to be applied with a gun—and it has to be applied all in one go. You can't patch it. When *Mistral* gets back to London, she'll have to be stripped and re-coated.'

Their conversation was being overheard by several other people in the lounge of the big hotel, and Nicolette was aware of faces turning to stare at the big bearded man who was so obviously furious with the little group at the corner table.

'How much is it going to cost?' asked Samantha.

'You can thank your lucky stars that my father's yard will do the job,' he snapped. 'After all, *Mistral* is his latest design. But you're going to be charged for the materials. And it's going to run into two or three thousand pounds all told.'

'I'm not paying that,' said Julian flatly. 'You can't prove that it was my fault—'

'Of course it was your fault! Twenty yachtsmen saw you run into me, Mitchell.'

'Did they?' A cunning look came into Julian's puffy eyes, and he leaned back, puffing at his cigar. 'You'll have to produce all these witnesses in court, Alex. In London.'

'Then you don't admit liability?' Alex asked quietly.

Samantha smiled, licking her lips. 'Of course he doesn't,' she said triumphantly. 'You'll have a hard job proving your case against Julian, Mr St Cloud. It's just your word, isn't it? And there are six of us who'll swear different.'

There was a tense pause, and once again Nicolette was afraid Alex St Cloud was going to strike Julian. But with a monumental effort of self-control, he kept his big hands on the table.

'Then you'd better contact your lawyer,' he said with soft menace, 'because St Cloud Construction will be suing you.'

'Go ahead,' Julian smiled. Once more, a hot flush of shame rose to Nicolette's face at their behaviour. She met Samantha's almond eyes bitterly. How adept they all were at saving their own skins, at protecting one another. It would have been the same, she was certain, had Pete Franklin been killed instead of merely badly hurt.

'I wonder if you know how much trouble you're causing me,' Alex grated. '*Mistral* was fresh from the boatyard, Mitchell. Do you know that? She hasn't even been sold yet.' He stared across the room with bitter, vacant eyes, almost talking to himself. 'She was on her sea trials. A brand-new boat. And you rich fools had to run into her with your pocket battleship!' He rose, staring at them with utter contempt in his grey eyes. 'We'll meet again, Mitchell. Now I have to go and find another crew member to get *Mistral* home. And God knows where I'm going to find one in this town.'

'Well, all the best, Alex,' grinned Julian, sipping from his Piña Colada. 'I'm sure you'll find someone.'

Alex stared at him with furious amethyst-grey eyes for a second, then said something unprintable, and turned on his heel.

'Well, really,' drawled Geraldine, her voice a husky purr, 'some people have no breeding at *all*.'

Nicolette's gin was suddenly sour in her throat. She put

the glass down firmly, picked up her bag, and walked out after Alex. The others paid her scant attention as she left, because they were laughing at Samantha's imitation of Alex's parting remark. She caught up with Alex in the foyer of the hotel, and took his arm. He spun round, ready to lash out, and she met his furious face as calmly as she could.

'You again?' he snapped. 'What the hell do you want?'

'I—I want to apologise for the way Julian and the others treated you, Alex—'

'Save your breath,' he said scornfully. 'I'm sick of listening to all your Belgravia accents.'

'Is your yacht—is she badly damaged?'

'She'll sail,' he said shortly. 'Though I'm not likely to find anyone to sail her in this damn town.'

'Can't *Mistral* be sailed by one person?' she asked gently.

'Not safely,' he said, looking her up and down with angry eyes. 'She needs at least two. Preferably three. Anyway, what do you care?'

'I feel responsible,' she said simply.

'You ought to,' he told her grimly. She fell into step beside him, and then paused with him at the big stainless-steel door of the hotel.

'Are you in a hurry to get back to Britain?' she asked.

'As it happens, yes. A hell of a hurry. There's a potential buyer for *Mistral* in London. Bjorn Olafsen—he's a big name in yacht racing. And he's in a hurry. He wants *Mistral* for the Trans-Atlantic Yacht Race, and if I can't get her back to London, and repaired, in twelve days, my father's going to lose the sale to his biggest rivals.'

'*Elsie* really has messed things up for you, hasn't she?'

she sighed. A colourful party of Kenyans in bright kaftans jostled past them.

'Not *Elsie*,' said Alex grimly. 'Her crew.'

'I'm sorry,' she said, no longer able to face those furious eyes, 'I can see that you hate me. I'll leave you in peace.' He stared at her for a few seconds as she turned to leave.

'*Mistral*'s the best thing my father ever built,' he said at last, the words coming slowly. Nicolette could suddenly see that he was a tired man, fighting through his exhaustion with indomitable will power. 'But it costs thousands of pounds to design and build a boat as advanced as *Mistral*, and my father's badly over-extended right now. It's very important for him to get some sales soon. And if Bjorn Olafsen takes *Mistral*—and shows the professionals what she can do—then all those months and years of work will start paying off. Yes, your friends have messed things up for me.'

'What are you going to do?' she asked quietly.

He shrugged. 'I don't have the slightest damned idea. Right now I'm arranging to have Pete flown back to England as soon as the doctors let him go. After that, I'll be sitting here, waiting for a replacement to materialise out of nowhere.' He turned to go.

'Alex—'

He stopped. 'What now?'

'Alex,' she said, not quite knowing why she was saying it, 'if I should happen to find someone who could go with you—is there anywhere I can phone you?'

'Yes,' he said, looking at her curiously. 'You can call me at the Yacht Club. Just ask for *Mistral*'s skipper.'

Nicolette nodded. 'Good luck,' she said, watching his tall figure stride off into the night. Julian Mitchell's guffaw floated out of the lounge, reaching her where she stood at the door. As if the sound had thrust her bodily out, she found herself strolling absently along the pavement through the crowd, her mind more or less blank. Mombasa by night was a happy, colourful city, thronged with a million smells and sounds. She bought an ice-cream cone from a street vendor, and strolled along the street, licking it, and staring thoughtfully into the shop windows, at shelves full of touristy wooden carvings and beads, various things made out of animal skins, piles of glossy, useless articles for Mum and Dad to take back to Dresden or Rome or Birmingham.

The esplanade was alive with music, the harbour like a Christmas display, the riding-lights and cabin-lights of the boats making brilliant squiggles in the water. The warm breeze carried the smells of strange spices and curries, and African rhythms poured sweetly from nightclubs and street bands. Nicolette's blonde hair and full-breasted figure drew whistles and a lot of harmless, impudent gallantry, but she did not mind. She felt safe here, safer than she would have done in certain areas of London. There was a happy, carefree feeling in the air that she wished she could join in with.

She sat at the foot of the old war memorial, gazing out across the dark bay and its firefly lights. As always, her thoughts were hovering around the subject of Mark Macmillan. The accident this afternoon, she felt, was going to drive a further wedge between them—she knew Mark was going to take Julian's side, no matter what the facts were. Mark and his friends always stuck together. It was a class thing, a network which linked people like Mark and Julian together to the exclusion of other people. Like herself.

Mark's world, she had begun to discover, was full of invisible trip-wires. But Mark was what he was, and he was not going to change to suit her. Had she lost his love? With a chill, empty feeling inside her, she wondered whether he might not have lost hers.

At least there was some consolation in the thought of getting back to work. She could lose herself in the patient details of her craft, the cleaning and restoration of precious paintings. She excelled in the meticulous work that could turn a near-ruined masterpiece into something beautiful and joy-giving again. Oil paintings were her speciality, and Nicolette Mercury was already a sought-after name in the art world. After her success with the famous Rubens there had been articles about her work in all the dailies, even a television interview. A maniac had torn a huge rent in the priceless painting with a knife, and the gallery had asked her to do what she could. It had taken her months of meticulous work; the endless stitching with tiny needles, the intricate work with resins and fillers. And finally, the retouching, the hardest part of all. She had worked across the smooth scar like a plastic surgeon, using soft oil pastels under a magnifying glass, trying to copy the exact shades and strokes of the great master. By the time she had finished, the scar was invisible, even at magnifying-glass range. The gallery staff had been almost tearful with gratitude, the general public impressed, and Nicolette had found herself a minor celebrity overnight. London Weekend Television had interviewed her on a news programme when the Rubens had gone back on show. After that, her temporary fame had vanished rapidly. But the commissions had kept rolling in. She had been able to leave the art firm which had employed her, and had set up a studio of her own in Knightsbridge (huge rent, but excellent address) and had been doing well. And had met Mark in his parents' home, while surveying a collection of mildewed second-rate watercolours that Mrs Macmillan seemed to think she might be able to turn into masterpieces by some magic or other.

Nicolette sighed, and stood up, dusting the seat of her dress. More than one man cast admiring looks at her trim calves as she walked slowly back; but the pretty girl with the beautiful, long blonde hair was in a sombre mood.

Back in her room, she lay on the bed, miserable. Much had changed over the past twenty-four hours, and she was not altogether sure why. It was as though she had been wearing rose-tinted spectacles, and someone had suddenly knocked them off.

She thought of the faces in the yacht that morning. Ugly, selfish, cowardly faces. She had known that they were superficial people, using a pretence of sophistication and charm to cover inadequate personalities. But she now saw them in a grimmer light still—as corrupt children, using their wealth and privilege to force a ruthless passage through other people's lives. There was nothing attractive about them at all.

On a sudden impulse, she picked up the bedside telephone and asked the switchboard to give her the International Operator. Then she asked for Mark's number in London. When his cultured tones broke through the silence, she knew she had phoned at the wrong moment. The edges of his voice were blurred with drink, and there was an aggressive note in his voice which she had come to dread over the past weeks.

'Mark? It's me.'

'Hullo, you. How's Kenya?'

She sighed, not wanting to talk to him after all. She hated talking to Mark when he was drunk; he was apt to want to confess things, usually things she would rather not have known.

'I just wanted to hear your voice,' she said lightly. 'I won't disturb you—'

'Nonsense.' She could hear him gulp at something. 'What's the latest news?'

She hesitated, then told him about the accident. He heard her out in silence, then asked aggressively, 'So? What did you expect Julian to do?'

'Well,' she sighed, not really wanting to discuss it at all, 'he could have admitted that he was in the wrong, for a start, which would have been more gentlemanly—'

'Since when are you such an expert on gentlemen?' he taunted, and she flushed, choosing to ignore him.

'—and in the second place, he does owe Alex the cost of repairs.'

'I see,' said Mark with a sharp note in his voice, 'so you're an expert on the law as well, are you?'

'I may not know anything about the law,' she said quietly, 'but I do know something about sailing. And Julian was in the wrong. No—worse. He was criminally negligent. *And* he was drunk.'

'Before you start chucking accusations around, just remember that Julian's given you a free holiday, Nicky. Don't bite the hand that feeds you, old girl.'

'I paid my own way,' she retorted. 'And you know I'd much rather have flown to Kenya in the first place—I didn't want to go on *Elsie*. And as for Julian, he might have killed Alex today!'

'*Alex?*' he parodied. 'You sound very pally with this blighter, whoever he is!'

'At least he's decent,' she rejoined, her temper beginning to rise. 'He saved my life in Serengeti, if you want to know.'

'Really?' Mark drawled in mock amazement, '*do* tell.'

She told him the story as impersonally as she could, and he grunted at the end of it.

'Huh—sounds to me as though you're rather falling in love with this paragon of virtue, my dear Nicky—are you?'

'You're drunk, Mark,' she said drily. 'And I don't think I want to talk to you any more.'

'Wait.' There was a long pause. When he spoke again, there was an odd, false note in his voice that puzzled her. 'Nicky, old girl, has anyone been talking to you about me?'

'All the time,' she said lightly. 'You're the main topic of conversation. Why?'

'Oh—well, it's nothing.'

'Mark,' she said patiently, 'what is it?'

'Well, I was just wondering whether you had some other—but no, it's nothing.'

'You're being infuriating, Mark,' she snapped. 'What the dickens are you driving at? Is something bothering you?'

'Well, I was rather wondering whether there was anything bothering *you*,' he replied mysteriously.

She sighed in exasperation. There was something on Mark's mind, she knew that plainly. And he was inviting her to dig it out of him—an old game of his, and one which had always seemed very tedious to her.

'Of course I'm bothered, Mark—I'm bothered about that accident. And I dread the thought of going home on *Elsie.*'

'Why, Nicky? Has—has something else happened?' he asked, a strange edge in his voice.

She frowned impatiently. 'What are you getting at?'

He hesitated. 'No one's said anything to you, then?'

'About what?' she asked, beginning to worry seriously now.

'Oh,' he laughed, a false sound that made her wince, 'you know—people gossip, don't they?'

'Why should anyone gossip about you?' she demanded.

'Oh, I don't know,' he said, sounding confused. He tried the laugh again. 'It was just a thought, Nicky—in case anyone's been talking about me—and Gerry—'

'Geraldine? And you?' Nicolette shook her head in bewilderment. 'What would there be to gossip about?'

'Are you trying to torment me?' he asked, his voice still edgy, and Nicolette realised that for some mad reason he thought she had found something out—something about Mark and Geraldine—

'Mark,' she said anxiously, 'have you and Geraldine had some kind of argument?'

'Scarcely an argument, old girl,' he said, laughing nervously again. 'Listen—it was all an accident, to begin with—it started that weekend in Scotland, when you thought we were out with the ponies—'

She stared blindly at the plush carpet, at her own pink-nailed toes, too numb to speak.

'You don't have to pretend, Nicky,' Mark said theatrically. 'I can guess what happened. That bastard Frank has always been jealous of me and Geraldine. It would be just like him to break the news to you—to get back at me. What did he say, exactly?'

'Mark,' she said, her voice almost a whisper, 'how long has this been going on?'

'I told you,' he said irritably. 'Since Scotland. Maybe a year now.'

'And you've been—sleeping together?'

'Don't be such a child,' he said drily. 'Of course we've been sleeping together.' In the silence that followed, he said rather nervously, 'Nicky? I mean—you and I weren't—well, weren't doing anything like that. A chap has to have *some* fun out of life.'

'You have nothing but fun,' she said, clenching the receiver in her hand. 'We were going to be married!'

'We can still get married,' he said, the insincerity making his voice brittle. 'If you want to.'

'*If I want to!*'

'I suppose you've teamed up with this chap St Cloud to get me back,' he said quietly. 'You don't have to do that, Nicky—'

'Get you back? You talk like a schoolboy!' she exclaimed furiously.

'You mean you haven't—well, given yourself to him?'

'Is that what you think of me?' she asked, unable to believe her ears.

'I wouldn't put it past you,' he said with a false laugh. 'You can be a little cat at times—'

'As a matter of fact,' she snapped bitterly, 'Alex *is* my lover, yes! And I'm going with him on *Mistral*!'

'Can I take it, then,' he said calmly, with a note of—was

it triumph? in his voice, 'that anything between us is now over?' Nicolette stared blindly at the phone as he droned on, his voice as dry and concise as a lawyer's, telling her that things had come to a certain pitch, that it would be immature to keep pretending, that adults should know when to call a halt, that—

'Mark,' she said, her voice shaking, 'you contrived this whole conversation, didn't you? You *wanted* me to know! You were just dying to tell me about this sordid little affair with Geraldine—'

'Steady on,' said Mark uncomfortably, and she could hear the guilt in his voice.

'If you wanted to get out of this relationship,' she said furiously, 'why didn't you just come out and say so? You didn't have to go to this length!'

'Look, Nicky, there's no sense in being childish—'

She slammed the phone down with a crash, buried her face in her hands, and burst into a flood of scalding tears.

When she had recovered a little, she snatched up the phone again, her mind whirling. Would Alex take her on? Probably not. In fact, definitely not. He had obviously associated her with the dissolute crew of *Elsie*. And she couldn't risk being turned down by him now. A mad, vague plan had begun to take shape in her mind. She called the switchboard again, and asked for the Mombasa Yacht Club.

Alex's voice was cold and hard.

'Yes?'

'I think I've found your crewman,' she said. 'When do you want to leave Mombasa?'

'As soon as possible, of course,' he replied. 'There's a

tide at three o'clock this morning, in fact. I could leave then—*Mistral's* practically seaworthy. Why?' Her heart jumped. Three in the morning—while it was still dark. There might be time—it might just work! She thought of Alex, assessing the penetrating power of those grey eyes. Could she possibly fool this man? Her stomach fluttered. Maybe just. Maybe just for a few hours. She cleared her throat.

'There's a young man we met in one of the waterfront bars. A student, I think. He mentioned that he was looking for a passage home. He'd been robbed,' she added, inventing freely, 'and he'd lost all his money.'

'Well,' he snapped, 'who is he? What's his name?'

'Oh—er—it was Timmy,' she said. 'Maybe it was Tommy, though—'

'It doesn't matter,' he said impatiently. 'Do you know where to find him?'

'Oh yes,' she beamed.

'Where?' he demanded.

'Well—er—' she floundered, 'he said he was going out to-night. I'm not sure where to. Would you like me to contact him when he gets back?'

'No, I'll speak to him,' he said, obviously thinking intently. 'Where is he staying?'

'He—er—well, I'm not sure of that, either. Look,' she said desperately, 'I'll get hold of him as soon as he gets back, and send him down to your yacht. Will that do?'

'I suppose it'll have to,' he said, after a pause. 'Look, this kid's not in any trouble, is he? Drugs, or something like that?'

'Oh no,' she exclaimed, 'nothing of that sort.'

'How do you know?'

'He didn't look the type,' she said firmly. 'But I know he was very eager to get a passage back.'

'Hmmm. Tell him I'll pay the flat Seamen's Union rate,' he said. 'And try and get him down to the yacht basin as soon as you see him. Okay?'

'Okay,' she said happily.

'If he gets there before three a.m., we'll sail at once. Got that?'

'I'll tell him,' Nicolette said solemnly. She was mentally making a list of the things she was going to need—would there be an all-night chemist somewhere in the city?

'Look,' said Alex, his tone slightly less hostile now, 'I've forgotten your name.'

'Nicolette Mercury.'

'That's right. They call you Nicky, don't they?'

'Sometimes,' she said. He could not know that she hated any abbreviation of her name, or that Mark had always insisted on 'Nicky', something she had resented from the start.

'Nicky—if you can get this Tommy or Timmy along to *Mistral* to-night, I'll be very glad.'

'I'll do my best,' she promised, grinning inwardly.

'Yes, well—I'm sorry if I was harsh with you—'

'I understand,' she said gently. 'I'll go and look for him now.'

With a hasty goodbye, she put the phone down and ran out to the lift, counting her money. Would she be able to pull it off? she wondered. It would be dark—that was on her side. And the deception would only have to last a few hours. Once they were out to sea, he would scarcely turn back again.

She found an open chemist's in the next street, snatched

up a wire basket, and began looking for the things she was going to need. Scissors, hair-dye, aspirins, some assorted cosmetics, sea-sickness tablets—she might need those on a big yacht, some glue . . .

With her arms full of her purchases, Nicolette ran back through the crowded streets to the hotel. In the lift, she twisted over her parcels to glance at her watch. Nearly ten-thirty. 'Damn!' she whispered. There was not very much time!

CHAPTER THREE

IT was two-thirty when the taxi finally nosed its way along the quayside, its headlights picking a path through the inky darkness that lay on the yacht basin. Alex St Cloud looked up from the charts he was surveying, his heart rising. Would this be a change in his luck?

A slight figure in a bulky anorak climbed out of the car, looked hesitantly around the silent yachts, and then caught sight of the hurricane lamp hanging over *Mistral*'s decks. He waved to Alex, paid the taxi, and then carried his bags over to the beautiful grey yacht. Alex turned the hurricane lamp up, shedding a pool of soft yellow light over the gangplank, and went to meet the new arrival, a rather slim boy.

'Mr St Cloud?' the boy asked, in a gruff voice. 'My name's Tommy Watson. Nicky sent me.'

'Hello there,' said Alex, surveying the lad dubiously in the dim light. Short black hair, a surprisingly delicate face, a rather comical black moustache. There was something familiar about the boy's stance.

'Haven't I seen you somewhere before?' he asked thoughtfully.

The boy shook his head hastily.

'Don't think so, guv'nor. 'Ere, is it true you're looking for crew?'

'Yes,' said Alex, looking the young man up and down.

'Have you had any experience with sailing boats?'

'Sure,' said the boy confidently. 'Me old man used to take me out in 'is sloop. When he was alive, that is. I know the basics, anyhow.'

Alex began to look happier. This somewhat effeminate-looking kid might be all right after all.

'Can you read a compass?'

'Pretty well. And I can cook and clean, too.' Alex's eyebrows rose. The boy cleared his throat hastily, and looked up at the radar bowl on the mast. 'I can read radar as well,' he said, more gruffly.

'Charts?'

'Like I said, guv, I know the basics. I'll soon pick up anything I don't know.'

'Hmmm.' Alex looked at the boy with growing interest. He really was rather slight-looking, almost girlish. 'I'm no millionaire, Tommy. All I can afford is the flat union rate.'

'That'll do me fine, guv,' the boy replied, in that curiously gruff voice. 'All I really want is me passage home.'

'You've cut things a bit fine. The tide'll be turning in—' Alex consulted his watch, '—in ten minutes. Can you leave right now? As you are?'

'Sure,' the boy replied, with a delightful grin. That moustache really was comical! No doubt the poor kid grew it to make himself look older and more masculine. But the gentle brown eyes that met his without flinching were steady enough; and though he was a slight figure, muffled in clothes that seemed too big for him, there was a determined quality about this boy that Alex was beginning to like. He glanced at the boy's grimy hands. They too were slender, almost delicate; but they also looked competent. A thought struck him.

'How old are you, Tommy?'

The boy looked confused. 'Er—twenty, guv.'

'Come off it,' said Alex quietly. 'You're not even eighteen. How old are you? Fifteen? Sixteen?'

'I'm seventeen, guv,' said the boy, 'straight up.' But Alex knew he was lying.

'You're in some kind of trouble, Master Watson, aren't you?' he asked kindly. 'What is it—police?'

'Nah,' said the boy anxiously, 'nuffink like that, skipper. I'm clean, I swear it. It's what you might call—er—family troubles.'

'What sort of family troubles?'

'Well, if you really want to know, guv, both me parents have died recently. There's only me Auntie Joan left—an' she's on the game an' all—'

'All right,' said Alex, his keen grey eyes suddenly compassionate, 'you don't have to say any more. I'm going to take you on, Tommy—no questions. Okay?'

'That's terrific!' exclaimed the boy, his voice breaking into a clear soprano. Alex felt sorry for him. Poor, homeless kid, so obviously delighted to have found a friend. 'Tommy,' he said, 'please don't call me "guv". My name's Alex. Or "Skipper" will do, if you prefer that.'

'Right you are, Skipper,' grinned the boy, showing beautiful white teeth. Once again, Alex thought there was something familiar about that smile—what was it? He grinned in return, and shook the boy's hand heartily. The boy winced. Poor kid, he really wasn't very strong.

'Are you going to be all right, Tommy?' he asked dubiously.

''Course I am, guv—er—Skipper. I'm as strong as an 'orse, honest I am.'

Alex turned away to hide a smile.

'We've got five minutes to catch the tide, Hercules. Get your bags stowed away in the for'ard cabin, and let's get weaving!'

'Aye aye, sir,' said Tommy with happy professionalism, and Nicolette scampered joyfully down to her cabin.

Mistral sailed out into a blood-red dawn, her sails filled with the early morning breeze that swept from Africa out to sea. The water glittered ahead of the slim grey yacht like a long sheet of molten silver, and Nicolette was filled with the beauty of it all. She obeyed Alex's instructions promptly and silently, and by six o'clock, Africa was merely a long purple smudge over to starboard. As the sun rose, the sea became a deep intense blue, and the sky changed to cobalt. It was soon hot, and the salt sea breeze had washed every trace of land-smell off the boat and its rigging.

The activity soon tailed off once *Mistral* was under way, and Nicolette went unbidden to the galley while Alex checked through his charts, and began to assemble the ingredients for breakfast. He looked up in surprise as she brought the steaming plate of bacon and eggs up to the bridge.

'That looks like a million dollars,' he grinned, taking the plate and tucking in. 'Where did you learn to cook?'

'I just picked it up,' she smiled. 'I more or less 'ad to cook, after Muvver died. Dad couldn't cook for monkey-nuts. God rest 'is soul,' she added piously.

Alex nodded, staring out to sea.

'My mother died when I was a kid,' he said. 'So there was just me and Dad—like you, I guess.'

'Really? What does your dad do for a living?' she asked, trying to keep her clear voice as gruff as possible.

'He designs boats,' Alex smiled. 'He designed this one, for instance.'

'Coo—and you, Skipper? Are you in the same line of trade?'

'No. Not quite, anyway. I design craft—but aircraft, not boats.'

'Garn!'

'It's true. I make executive jets for the super-rich, helicopters, that sort of thing.'

'I'll bet *you're* rich,' she said, patting her moustache, which was beginning to itch like fury. When should she reveal herself? Not until they were a good long way up the coast, she decided.

'No, I'm not rich, Tommy,' Alex smiled. 'I make a living, that's all. But I hope things will improve soon, once I've paid off all my overheads. Look, why don't you take off that anorak,' he added. 'It's going to get as hot as hell pretty soon, and you'd be best off in a T-shirt.'

'I—er—yes,' she muttered, feeling a flush rise to her cheeks. 'In a minute. I've got a bit of a cold, actually, and—'

'Why didn't you say so?' said Alex, putting his plate down and rising with a look of concern. 'I'll get you something. Got a headache?'

'Er—no. I mean yes, that is—'

'Poor kid! Here, take two of these.'

Reluctantly, Nicolette swallowed the aspirins with the

mug of water he passed her. He took the mug to throw the remainder of the water out, and then stopped rigid, peering into the mug with an expression of astonishment. Something was floating in the water, something black and hairy.

Her moustache.

Alex's eyes met hers in amazement, and then his face went cold and hard.

'What the hell is this?' he rasped.

Nicolette cleared her throat nervously. At least she could now shed the gruff voice that had belonged to 'Tommy.'

'I think I'd better explain, Mr St Cloud—' she began.

'My God,' he interrupted. '*You*! Nicolette Mercury!'

'I'm afraid so. I—'

He stepped over to her, his face grim with anger.

For a moment she thought he might strike her, and she flinched away. He grasped her arms with unbelievably strong hands, and she gasped.

'What kind of joke is this?' he snarled. 'Who put you up to this game, you little vixen?'

'Nobody put me up to it,' she gasped. 'You're hurting my arms—'

'I mean to. What the devil do you mean, deceiving me like this?'

'I knew you'd never take me on if I suggested it,' she said. 'Please let me go!'

'Let you go?' He shook her furiously. 'I ought to chuck you to the sharks!'

'I only wanted to help you,' she said nervously. 'After all, you said I owed you a favour—remember?'

'A favour? I wasn't that desperate,' he snapped, thrusting her away. 'Right, run that foresail down, Miss Mercury. We're heading back to Mombasa.'

'Please wait,' she begged, running after him. 'There's no point in going back now—'

'Yes, there is. I'm going to put you back ashore and give you back to your friends, little stowaway!'

'They'll have left by the time we get back,' she said urgently. 'And I'm not going aboard *Elsie* again anyway.'

'I don't care where you go, as long as you go off my ship,' he retorted. 'If you won't take that sail down, I'll do it myself.'

'You can't even see past your own anger, can you?' she said quietly. 'You're so cocksure of your own correctness. But what are you going to do when you've put me ashore? Sit rotting in Mombasa for weeks? Don't you owe your father something?'

'Let me decide what I owe, and to whom,' Alex said icily. 'I'm not going to risk my father's property with a spoiled puppy like you!'

'You've seen what I can do already this morning,' she reminded him. 'That part of the story was true—I do know the basics of sailing.'

'Yes, I've had ample evidence of your skill,' he sneered, pointing to the smashed planks on the deck.

'I wasn't at the wheel of that boat, Mr St Cloud,' she said, her own temper beginning to rise. 'Why take it out on me? You said yourself that I wasn't their sort. And if you want to know, I was trying to make Julian stop when he hit your yacht.'

'You weren't very successful, were you?'

'That wasn't my fault,' she snapped. 'I did my best.'

'If that's your best,' he jeered, 'I'd hate to see what you're going to do with my boat!'

'Then take me back to Mombasa,' she rejoined hotly. 'Rot there, if you insist on it.'

'I'd sooner rot in Mombasa than be sunk by you,' he snarled, his grey eyes furious as he towered over her.

'I don't need lessons from anyone in sea-safety,' Nicolette said quietly. 'That part of the story was also true. My father was drowned in the Channel five years ago.'

He stared at her, the anger fading in his eyes.

'I'm sorry,' he said. 'I didn't know that.'

'And he did teach me to sail when I was a kid,' she said, in the same quiet voice. 'I really could help you, Mr St Cloud.'

He stared at her, taking in the short dyed hair and the clumsy anorak which she had worn to conceal her figure. Her hair, he noticed for the first time, had been clumsily hacked, as though cut in front of a mirror in haste; and she had used brown foundation-cream to make her face look tanned, the skin rough.

'You've ruined your beautiful fair hair,' he said inconsequentially. 'Will that dye wash out?'

'I don't know,' she admitted wryly.

He stared at her, his eyes suspicious.

'Why do you want to help me, Miss—er—Mercury?'

'Because I was on *Elsie*,' she said simply. 'And I'd like to repay you for some of the damage we did. Especially as it doesn't seem likely that Julian Mitchell intends to meet his obligations. But also because I do owe you a favour. You'll never know how glad I was to see your Range Rover appear out of the rain that day. I don't think I've ever been so scared in all my life.'

'What about Mitchell—and your other friends? I presume they're as much in the dark about your stupid little scheme as I was?'

'I left a note for them,' she said, meeting his eyes calmly. 'I don't think they'll miss me much.'

'And dear Mark? What's he going to say when he hears about this—this charade of yours?'

'As a matter of fact—' she began, then stopped herself, her eyes dark. There was a pause, and then she sighed. 'I don't care what he says,' she told him, the words leaving her throat as though they had been fish-bones. In the silence, the wind whistled quietly through the rigging. The sun was already high by now, and she was sweltering in the anorak she had stolen from Julian Mitchell's room. Alex St Cloud stared at her, his grey eyes thoughtful, his savage face intent.

'It's going to take a lot longer to get back on *Mistral* than it would have done on *Elsie*,' he said drily. Nicolette met the hard challenge of his eyes without feeling.

'My job will be waiting,' she said. 'And if you don't take me back to Mombasa, you'll get *Mistral* back on time.'

Then she knew he was going to agree. He stared at her with beautiful slate-grey eyes that seemed to be seeing her for the first time.

'There doesn't seem to be much I can do about it,' he said bitterly. 'You might as well try and undo some of the harm your rich mates have done, I suppose.' She tried to suppress the grin of triumph that rose to her lips. 'And for God's sake try and do something about that hair,' he snapped. 'You weren't too bad as Tommy Watson. As Nicolette Mercury you're hideous!'

'I'll do my best,' she promised, and smiled—a gentle smile that made her look lovely, despite the absurd cropped hair. But Alex St Cloud was impervious to any beauty that might lie in Nicolette's face.

'You're under sufferance,' he said, turning a broad back to her dismissively. 'Just don't put a foot wrong. Got that?'

'Aye, aye,' she said, chastened. 'Have you finished your breakfast—Skipper?'

In her own cabin, Nicolette examined her hair ruefully. Perhaps the black dye would come out, but the homemade haircut she had given herself as 'Tommy Watson' was a mess. Her feminine impulses were re-emerging, now that her little deceit had had its effect. She was, after all, going to be in close contact with an extremely attractive man for the duration of a longish sea voyage. She thought of Alex's tall, powerful figure, the level grey eyes that seemed to look straight through her. He was undeniably 'dishy', as Geraldine would have put it; yet it was hard to tell what he really looked like under that fierce black beard. She stuck her head in the basin, ran a little water into it, and proceeded to lather her poor black locks.

Several vigorous washes removed the last of the dye, and her hair was revealed in the honey gold of its original tint—a beautiful, rich colour that her father had always called 'wild honey'. But it was sadly hacked. For the first time, she felt a pang for her lovely long tresses. In the anxiety and excitement of disguising herself for Alex, Nicolette had scarcely thought about her hair. She had simply snipped it off, and thrust the heavy golden stuff into her waste-basket. She had not even kept a lock of it. For a few moments she felt like crying, as she surveyed her bizarre haircut; it was like the punk fashions of a few years back, only softer and fluffier.

With a heavy heart, she took up the scissors and set about neatening it. The basin was lined with gold clippings by the time she had finished. She had reduced the disorganised haircut of last night to a short—a very short—mop of blonde half-curls. The result was far from beautiful. She looked like a street urchin, she decided, some *gamine* from the streets of any big city. At least the curls all lay together now, catching the light with their usual glint—but oh, how short it was! Thinking of her lost locks, she shook her head dismally at her own reflection, and went to pull on a T-shirt and a pair of jeans. Then she ventured up into the sunshine on deck.

The wind had risen slightly, and Alex was hauling down the spinnaker. Nicolette moved beside him quietly to help, slackening the guy-rope for him as he lowered the big sail, which was beating powerfully in the wind. Out of the corner of her eye, she watched the tracery of muscle along his fore-arms as he tied the sail into a long, neat bundle. His hands were powerful, but extraordinarily beautiful—the fine, strong hands of an artist or a surgeon. He tied the last knot with a grunt, and then turned to face her. His eyes flicked to her hair.

'I'm glad you got that filthy paint out,' he said grimly. 'Why you had to cut all that hair off, though, I'll never know. Couldn't you have tied it up and hidden it under a cap?'

'I never thought of that,' she said ruefully.

'No,' he retorted sourly, 'you wouldn't have.' He looked at her, his grey eyes inscrutable, and then beckoned. 'Come—I want to run the mizzen out.' She followed him to the foremast, and as they hauled up the triangular sail, his eyes met hers with an awareness that jolted her in her solar plexus.

'Miss Mercury, I trust there's no—' He paused, holding the guy taut, '—no romantic nonsense in that cropped head of yours?'

'What do you mean?' she asked, puzzled.

'I mean,' he said coolly, 'I hope you didn't weasel your way on board this boat because of any foolish sentimental attraction to me?'

'Certainly not,' she said, her colour rising. He clipped the thin steel cable into its bolt and looked at her drily.

'I'm glad to hear it,' he said. 'That would have been an unnecessary complication.'

'I'm sure it would have,' she retorted, her face pink. 'Do you have much of that sort of trouble, Mr St Cloud?'

'It's been known to crop up,' he said calmly. A mocking grin appeared on his face, and she caught the glint of white teeth through the black curls of his beard. 'But I'm not in the market for romantic attachments, Miss Mercury. Is that understood?'

'Perfectly,' she gasped, her breath taken away by his calm arrogance.

'Good. It's nearly one-thirty, Tommy Watson. Time for lunch, don't you think?'

Mistral sailed on through the afternoon, a grey gull drifting along the glittering waves. She was more or less sailing herself now, running before the wind with full sails, her elegant prow slicing through the bright water cleanly and smoothly. Always, to her left, Nicolette was conscious of the long purple line of Africa. They were close enough to land to be visited by seabirds, and a constant escort of big white gulls followed them, drifting past *Mistral*'s tall sails with bright eyes alert for any scraps. Nicolette threw the remains of their lunch on to the white wake of the yacht, and the birds dipped for the morsels with harsh, haunting cries. Her thoughts turned once or twice to Mark, Julian, and the others, but she resolutely shut such topics off. She would wait to cross those stiles when she met them.

Alex's words earlier in the afternoon had hurt and disturbed her. After studying the charts for the area they were in, he had pulled off his shirt, and was lying on the foredeck in the afternoon sun, his magnificent torso a rich mahogany colour in the harsh light. From time to time she stole glances at him, noting the flat stomach, the broad chest with its husky triangle of dark hair that tapered so excitingly down over his stomach. The journey ahead was a long one—round the horn of Africa, up Suez, across the Mediterranean, and through the straits of Gibraltar. What sort of journey had she let herself in for?

She studied Alex covertly. There was so little spare flesh on his body that she could see the hard sculpture of his stomach muscles; yet he was a big man, powerfully built. That body must be solid muscle, she reflected, hard as the ruthless body of a barracuda. And there was something of the predator's savage anger about him, too. He was a fierce, impatient personality, his inner power often well concealed behind a deceptively gentle manner. Was she going to be able to cope with Alex St Cloud? There was no answer to her question.

The sun sank slowly in the west, filling the sky with glory. They ate quietly in the crimson glow, the world utterly at peace, but for the eerie voices of the gulls and the secret-whispering sea.

One by one the stars came out, pinpoints of diamond light against a dark velvety blue. The moon was nearly full—not an icy white English moon, but a rich orb of finest gold, glowing brightly among the lesser lights. Alex leaned back against the wheelhouse, gazing up at the moon with calm eyes.

'They say the moon is a virgin,' he said quietly. 'It's easy to think that in Europe, isn't it? But here, off the coast of Africa, it's not a virgin at all, is it? Or should I say she?' He looked up speculatively. 'She's a rich, beautiful woman, ready for love.' Nicolette sat silent, not knowing what to say. He looked at her, and in the dim light she saw the ironic glint in his grey eyes. 'Or so the poets would have us believe, anyway,' he said drily. 'I'm going to light the riding-lights.' He rose in a fluid movement that was characteristic of the man's animal grace, and went to ignite the red and green lights that would burn on *Mistral*'s mast during the hours of darkness. Nicolette washed the dishes, wondering about him, and then checked the compass against the course he had laid out. When he came back, he tapped the map on the chart table with a lean forefinger.

'We're going to be running into the Margherita Reefs pretty soon,' he told her. 'I'm going to take *Mistral* as close inshore as I can. I'd rather sail this side of the reefs than the seaward side.'

She nodded her understanding, and he spun the wheel to take the grey yacht towards the shore.

The vast land mass of Africa loomed gradually closer in the moonlit night. Nicolette stood next to Alex on the bridge, close enough to him to feel the warmth of his body. The night was like velvet, a deep blue African night; and as they neared the coast, the smell of Africa came to them on the breeze, a haunting, indefinable smell of campfires and aromatic plants—a smell that Nicolette knew she was never going to forget.

'What country is this?' she asked softly.

'Somalia,' he told her. 'You'll be able to see the shore soon.'

And in the stillness of the night, the low roar of the surf on the beach came softly. Soon they were close enough to see the long line of palm trees that fringed the beach, a ghostly silver streak in the moonlight.

Now she could see the white lines of the breakers, rushing up on to the beach half a mile away. *Mistral*'s full sails carried them swiftly towards the coast, and when the yacht was within clear view of the moonlit beach, Alex turned her forward, and set a course north, along the line of the African coast.

Bewitched by the incredible beauty of the scene, Nicolette leaned on the polished brass rail in the stern, and watched the coast drift by in the peaceful night. There was no sign of life anywhere on the long coast, not even the red glow of a campfire. She and Alex might have been the only two creatures living in all that solitude. The yacht drifted slowly on, past a cape, and along the long, straight line of the beach. The smell of the land was in her nostrils again, and she wondered whether it was preferable to the clean, salty sea-smell, the smell that was of nothing at all, that the air carried out at sea.

Alex came to stand next to her for a moment.

'We'll have to take some kind of watches,' he said. 'We'll get that worked out to-morrow. It's not really necessary, but I like to be safe.'

Nicolette nodded, and turned to watch the land drift by. She could discern the coconut palms that grew in huge groves along the beaches, and here and there an open stretch of savannah, studded with the inevitable thorn trees. How remote she was now from that weird afternoon in Serengeti, when she had ventured out of her car into the great unknown of Africa, alone and afraid. In this warm still night, she was deeply at peace, tranquil as the sighing sea on which they rode. How long would it last? she wondered wryly. She was too intelligent not to have recognised that there was a germ of truth in Alex's accusation of the afternoon. She *was* attracted to him— very strongly. It was not simply because he had come so providentially to her rescue in the game reserve, nor because of the accident in Mombasa harbour—it was because of what he was, a magnificent, beautiful, free spirit; as free and proud as the yacht that carried them so swiftly over the dancing sea.

She stared unseeingly into the velvety night, unaware of the millions of diamond-like stars that spangled the tropical sky overhead. She was thinking of Alex, of Mark, of herself, of all the strange paths that had led her, unwittingly, to this night on the sea under the stars.

A distant sound penetrated her reverie, a faint cough that seemed to drift on the breeze. At first she thought it must be Alex, but then she heard it again—a rough barking roar that for some reason raised the hackles on the back of her neck. It seemed to be coming from the shore. She turned to the wheelhouse, where Alex was plying dividers over the chart by the light of the hurricane lamp.

'Alex, come and listen to this.'

As he stepped out on to the deck, the sound came again,

a faint roar from the land. Alex cocked his head, his eyes intent.

'What is it?' she whispered. The roar was joined by a second one now, and Alex suddenly grinned, his teeth glinting in the light.

'Let's go and see,' he said, striding over to the wheel. 'Your safari may not have finished yet—if you're lucky.' She stared across at the land as he brought *Mistral* steadily into the shore. The breakers grew closer and louder.

'Is it safe?' she called nervously.

'Yes—she draws very shallow. Keep your eyes on the beach.'

'What am I looking for?' she asked apprehensively.

'Lions,' he said succinctly.

Startled, she turned back to the beach. They were so close now that Nicolette could see the palm trees waving gently in the night breezes, the moonlight glittering on the pebbles on the beach. Again, the coughing roar came to them, louder now, and Nicolette's skin rose in gooseflesh. There was something deeply disturbing about that sound, here under the stars. Thank God they were on a yacht, and not on the lonely beach! As if reading her thoughts, Alex laughed.

'It's supposed to be frightening,' he said. 'They use that noise when they hunt—to frighten the game in the direction they want. Quiet now—and keep your eyes peeled.'

And then she saw them. Her blood froze, half in terror, half in a thrill of delight. Two big lions, walking slowly from between the palm trees on to the beach.

She turned, speechless, but Alex had seen them too. Silently, he let down the big sail, and then slipped the anchor overboard. It fell with a faint splash into the sea.

Transfixed, Nicolette watched the lions stroll across the sand, barely two hundred yards away. Under the moonlight, their coats were silver-gold. She thought she could even see the amber lights of their eyes. As she watched, three more lionesses came slowly out of the dark palm-groves to join their mates on the sand. Alex came quietly up to the rail next to her, and they watched in marvelling silence.

The big creatures rolled slowly in the sand, the males shaking their shaggy manes. Like huge cats, they played, batting one another with paws that could shatter bones, rolling in the soft sand under the moon. Nicolette's heart ached with the beauty of the scene—it was fantastic, the fabulous vision of some savage poet. The magical light gave the picture an unreal, dreamlike quality. The softly-crashing breakers made a fitting musical score for the majestic games of the lions, and the dark blue curtain of the night surrounded them. From time to time their coughs and grunts reached the yacht on the warm breeze. Nicolette and Alex watched, spellbound.

Mistral tugged at her sea-anchor, and the waves thrust her onwards; but they were so silent that the big animals on the shore were completely unaware of their presence. In the moonlight, they might have been cats playing innocently, five lithe, sleek bodies that twisted and rolled with the agility of their kind. Only a short stretch of surf separated them from the yacht, which lay like a great silent gull on the dark water, waiting to fly on.

Then, as slowly as they had come, the big cats made their way back into the palm trees, calling to one another in their rough voices from time to time. As the lions disappeared back into the darkness, Nicolette slowly became aware that her hand was aching. She looked down. It was clasped in Alex's. In the darkness their eyes met, hers big and soft, his dark and unfathomable. Then he released her hand, and turned to haul up the anchor.

'I want that spinnaker up,' he said matter-of-factly, and she stepped next to him to haul up the huge sail again. His hard shoulder bumped hers casually. As casually as though she had been part of the machinery on the deck. It was as though that strange interlude had never happened. She turned back wonderingly to stare at the shore. The silvery beach was silent, as deserted as an empty stage.

'Sightseeing's over,' said Alex shortly. 'Let's get going.'

The wind filled *Mistral*'s tall gull's-wing sail, and the grey yacht leaped eagerly forward against the sea.

CHAPTER FOUR

By midday of the next day they were rounding the horn of
Africa, and turning past the sandy, palm-covered island of
Abd al Kuri into the Gulf of Aden, the steel-blue water-
way that would lead them into the Red Sea. It had become
baking hot, and they were both slightly breathless in the
heat. Alex had stripped to a faded pair of shorts, and his
magnificent body gleamed with sweat as he hauled up
every spare stitch of canvas they had, in order to take
advantage of the slight breeze. Nicolette, too hot even for
jeans and T-shirt, had stripped to her violet bikini, and as
they secured the last guy-rope, she sat back on the deck,
gasping. Alex wiped wearily the sweat off his brow. He
had borne the brunt of the work, with his superior strength
and co-ordination, and his body was literally dripping.

She smiled up at him.

'Like me to hose you down?' she suggested.

'Please.'

She hauled the fire-fighting equipment out of its locker,
tossed the rubber hose into the water, and switched on the
pump, so that a stream of seawater shot out of the nozzle
she was holding. She played the stream of water across
Alex's broad back as he gasped with the cold shock of it. It
was a crude but effective means of staying cool in the
oven-like atmosphere of the Gulf. Even the Red Sea would
be preferable to this, as the wind would blow cool air from
the land across them. Clean and shiny-wet, Alex took the

71

hose from her and returned the favour. Nicolette pirouet-
ted ecstatically in the fine spray, remembering summer
days in her childhood when her father had done this for
her in the little garden in Surrey. Cool at last, they
retreated into the shade of the wheelhouse. Alex's eyes
glanced at her slender, full-breasted figure.

'I don't know how I was ever so stupid as to fall for your
disguise,' he said drily. She flushed, and turned to towel
her ridiculously short hair dry. At least her cropped curls
were cool in this blazing noonday sun; her long, heavy
tresses would have been unbearable. She peered at her
dim reflection in the mirror over the compass box. An elfin
face looked back at her with gentle brown eyes.

'I had no idea my ears stuck out so much,' she said
wistfully, wishing she looked more like Greta Garbo, and
less like Peter Pan.

'You should have thought of that before you were so
stupid,' Alex retorted. He looked at her critically. 'You
never had much to recommend you, apart from your hair.
And now that's gone.' She silently pulled on a towelling
shirt, and went into the galley to prepare something light
for lunch.

As they sailed towards the straits of Bab el Mandeb,
they were meeting more traffic on the bright water. They
had overtaken a succession of Arab dhows since dawn,
oddly-shaped boats with uplifted prows and huge, leath-
ery sails. As they ate their snack in silence, they found
themselves among a small flotilla of Arab boats, manned
by lean, dark-skinned men in white pyjama-like gar-
ments.

Finishing his food, Alex went up on to the bridge to keep
a look-out, and Nicolette found herself with time heavy on

her hands. She glanced up at him, a commanding figure keeping a careful eye on the waters ahead, and decided that she must find something to occupy herself with over the hot afternoon. She sat herself down to polish the nautical instruments, complicated affairs of brass and crystal. Lost in her work, she sat dreaming over the sextants and chronometers for almost an hour, until Alex came down from the bridge, and stood tall in the doorway.

'Something's just occurred to me—this fiancé of yours—Mark, was it?'

'Yes?'

'Have you told him where you are?'

'I—' she hesitated. 'No, actually, I haven't.'

'How do you expect him to know, then?' he asked sharply, his grey eyes watchful.

'I—I thought Julian Mitchell would explain,' she faltered. 'I left him a note—'

'You left Julian Mitchell to explain? And what do you think he's going to tell your precious boy-friend?'

'Why,' she said nervously, looking up at the handsome, bearded face, 'that you needed an extra crew member, and that I'd chosen to go with you . . .' She tailed off. His face was thoughtful.

'What does this Mark do for a living?'

'He's a stockbroker,' she said. 'Why?'

'He works on the Exchange, then?'

'The Stock Exchange in London, yes. But why?'

'Because I can raise them on the radio,' he said. 'I'm going to have a word with your Mark. What's his other name?'

'Macmillan. But why—'

'What do you think friend Julian is going to tell him?' he

sneered. 'After your bizarre prank, and after the little argument I had with him in Mombasa, don't you think this is his ideal opportunity to hit back at me?'

'What do you think he'll say?' she asked anxiously.

Alex put on a savage imitation of Julian's languid drawl. 'She met this yachtsman chappie, don't you know, and the next thing she was jumping into bed with him—'

'No!' she yelped.

'—and so, of course, she's run off with him on his boat,' he concluded. 'Well, I'm going to get hold of Mark right now—and then you can explain exactly what the position is. Right?'

'Alex, no,' she protested nervously. 'I don't want—'

'What you want is of no importance,' he interrupted. 'I'm not having myself compromised for the sake of your little jokes.'

'But let me explain—I didn't—'

'I'm going to call him up on the radio,' he said, walking up the companionway.

'Alex,' she called, running after him, 'please don't—'

He turned to her severely.

'Don't you think it would be fairer on the poor guy to let him know? He'll be imagining all kinds of things.'

She followed him helplessly up to the bridge. The massive radio set was on one of the chart tables, and Alex sat down in front of the complex black machine, and began calling London.

'Alex,' Nicolette tried a last time, 'you don't have to speak to Mark. I can explain what—'

'Your explanations are a little too plausible,' he said drily. 'This is *Mistral* calling London, *Mistral* calling London . . .' Within a few minutes, he had established contact with the London radio centre, and had asked them to patch a telephonic link through to the Stock Exchange. Calls such as this from yachts all over the world were common fare for the Stock Exchange switchboard operators; they were quite used to clients calling them from various glamorous and unusual locations across the globe.

Nicolette stood silently next to Alex as he waited, the microphone in his hand, for the switchboard girl to locate Mark Macmillan. Her heart was beating painfully fast. Why hadn't she told Alex the truth? Suddenly Mark's cultured voice crackled out of the radio set.

'Hello, *Mistral*? Mark Macmillan here. Who's calling, please?'

'This is Alexander St Cloud,' Alex said clearly. 'Listen to me, Macmillan, your fiancée is on board this boat— Nicolette Mercury.'

'Ah,' said Mark, his voice changing in that subtle way she knew so well. 'So that's who you are. What do you want?'

'I want to explain the situation,' said Alex quietly.

'Oh, you don't have to explain anything, old chap,' said Mark's genteel voice with maddening good humour. 'I quite understand—you've taken a fancy to my fiancée— my *ex*-fiancée, I should say—so you simply loaded her on board your dinghy, and sailed off into the sunset. Is that right?'

'No, that's not right,' Alex said grimly. 'Nicolette got on board by a trick—'

'Did she now?' said Mark sarcastically. 'You're a lucky man, Mr St Cloud—*I* could never get her to turn that trick. Perhaps you were more forceful?'

'Look, Macmillan—has Julian Mitchell been in contact with you?'

'As a matter of fact he has,' drawled the urbane voice. 'He tells me you rammed his boat, doing a considerable amount of damage. You were, I believe—how shall we say—under the influence of spiritous liquors?'

'That's a lie!' exclaimed Nicolette hotly, unable to contain herself.

'Is that my dear ex-fiancée?' asked Mark calmly. 'Nice to hear from you, Nicky. What's Mr St Cloud's bed like?'

'Look here, Macmillan,' snapped Alex angrily, 'you're jumping to conclusions. I haven't touched your girl. And if that swine Mitchell has implied that she and I are having some kind of affair, then he's an even bigger liar than I took him for!'

'Julian has been giving me some of the details,' said Mark languidly. 'But I didn't need his information to get the full picture. I'm a very busy man this morning, Mr St Cloud—can we cut this rather tedious conversation short?'

'What do you mean by that last remark?' Alex demanded in an icy voice.

'Didn't you know? I'm afraid your new floozy has already spilled the beans, old chap.'

'Nicolette? What the hell—'

'Oh, please don't play the innocent,' drawled Mark self-righteously. 'She phoned me the night you two left Mombasa to tell me the whole sordid story.'

'*What?*'

'You two seem to have got your stories mixed, old chap. Look, talking to you is giving me rather a pain at the moment. I'm going to ring off now. And please don't ring me back again—either of you.'

'Macmillan—!' snapped Alex, but he was gone. He slammed the microphone down on the table and spun in his chair to face Nicolette with blazing eyes. 'What the hell is all *this*?' he demanded furiously. 'Did you phone Mark and tell him we were having—some sort of relationship?'

'Alex,' she began, twisting her hands nervously, 'please let me explain.'

'I think you'd better,' he said, rising and looming over her. 'I've had just about enough of you and your insane schemes. Why did you tell him I was your lover?'

She looked unhappily at his fierce face. 'It just slipped out,' she said awkwardly.

'How the hell could a statement like that just slip out?' he snapped.

'Well,' she began, 'I was so upset about everything in Mombasa, Alex—so I phoned Mark and told him the whole story. We—well, we haven't been getting on too well lately. Something had come between us. We were both upset and confused—please believe me, Alex. That's why I came to Serengeti on my own in the first place—to give Mark a breathing space. He said he needed—'

'Spare me the details of your domestic arrangements, for God's sake! What happened when you phoned him in Mombasa?'

'He—he—well, he chose that particular evening to inform me that he'd been having an affair with one of our friends. Geraldine—you met her.'

'Who the hell is Geraldine?' he shrugged.

'The dark girl on the boat—the one with the diamond earrings.'

'Ah,' he said drily, 'the one who looks at all the men like a French tart?'

'That sounds like her,' said Nicolette with a touch of bitterness.

'I'm beginning to understand why you crept on board my yacht,' Alex said angrily, watching her with an unforgiving face. 'You wanted to get your spiteful little revenge on them all, didn't you?'

'I thought you might think that,' she said quietly. 'But it's not true. Anyway, Mark told me he and Geraldine had been meeting for months—'

'I'm not really interested,' he snapped. 'Dear God, you're a pretty lot of innocents, aren't you?'

'If you like,' she said quietly. 'But believe it or not, I was badly hurt. And Mark seemed to think that I'd found out about his little—arrangement with Geraldine. And that I was . . .' she faltered to a halt.

'That you were hopping into my bed for a spot of revenge?' he suggested grimly. She nodded. 'I see. And naturally, you confirmed that?'

'I was so upset, Alex. I didn't mean to use you like that. It just came out, with all the hurt inside me—'

'Oh, please,' he snapped, 'don't start playing the tragic heroine—I couldn't stand it!' He turned abruptly away from her, and gazed out over the late afternoon that was turning the Gulf of Aden into a sheet of beaten copper. 'You've played me for a sucker,' he said, his voice soft and menacing. 'Right from the start. I was a very convenient way out for you, wasn't I? A way out of a holiday you weren't enjoying—'

'No, Alex—'

'—and then a way out of a relationship that was beginning to bore you—'

'That's not true!' she cried. 'I loved Mark—' She

stopped, her mind whirling. *Loved?* Her eyes met his for a fraction of a second, and he smiled, a bitter little quirk of the mouth that burned her like acid.

'Go on,' he said silkily. 'I'm quite enjoying the performance.'

'I—' a lump had formed in her throat, and she gulped it back miserably. 'I didn't mean it to turn out like this, Alex—'

'You mean you didn't intend me to find out all the lies you'd been telling about me?'

'That's not what I meant. I didn't set out with the idea of using you. I meant to help you, to repay you in some way. I didn't mean to drag you into my troubles with Mark.'

'Didn't you?' He stared at her, contempt mingling with disbelief in his smile.

'I don't suppose it matters what I say, anyhow,' she said bitterly. 'You wouldn't believe me, would you?'

'No,' he said calmly, 'I wouldn't believe you now. From now on, Miss Mercury, when you say no, I'll know you mean yes.' He turned and looked out of the Perspex window ahead. Across the shimmering sea, a long line was appearing on the horizon.

'That's Ras Khanzira ahead,' he said. 'To use the words of your late fiancé, can we cut this rather tedious conversation short? I'm going to stop in Djibouti to-night to pick up fuel. It's somewhat cheaper in this part of the world,' he explained drily. 'Let's get back to work.'

'Alex —'

He stopped, turning to her with impatient eyes. 'Yes?'

'I don't want to be your enemy.'

'You're not my enemy,' he said in scorn. 'You simply don't matter a damn to me. Satisfied?'

The night was smoulderingly hot, and despite her short hair, Nicolette was too warm for comfort. The wild, high sound of Arab music drifted across the bay from Djibouti, and the harbour, even at night, was swarming with activity. *Mistral* was moored near the huge petroleum bowsers on the quayside, and the thick umbilical pipe that swayed from them to her sleek grey side was pumping fuel into her tanks. They had not used *Mistral*'s engines yet, but she knew that in the Red Sea they would probably run out of favourable winds, and would have to rely on their engines. She fanned herself with a paperback novel she had been idly reading, listening to the shouts of the Arab workmen. Alex was somewhere on the quayside, superintending the refuelling process. Nicolette slumped back on the settee in the wheelhouse, feeling her shirt sticking wetly to her back. She thought of English frosts and cool vistas of snow across the gentle landscape. She would never curse the cold weather again, she decided miserably. At sea, the heat was tolerable, even delicious; but in this decidedly smelly port, among the shimmering fumes of diesel fuel and a heady, industrial odour of ships, machinery and oil, the heat was horrific. Djibouti itself was a sprawling mass of dingy lights, crawling across a flattish hill, and she eyed it with disfavour. The wailing Arab music seemed to be incessant, like the sound of the sea.

Her relations with Alex, on the other hand, were little short of glacial. The few remarks he had addressed to her since the disastrous telephone call to London had chilled the hot air in the cabins as though a freezer door had been opened. Which was ironic, Nicolette thought wryly, because she was growing closer to him than ever. She could not help admiring the sure, economical power with which he ran the boat. He cared for *Mistral* with a deep passion, that was obvious, his instinct for the grey yacht's moods as certain as a lover's for his mistress's flights of temperament. She had longed to ask him about his father, about his own work, but normal conversation was scarcely possible. His conversation, in fact, had been limited to sharply-barked orders, which she had obeyed instantly.

She ran her fingers wearily through her cropped hair. Alex was no ordinary man, and no woman could be blamed for falling slightly in love with him. Yet she was sure that she had not done so. She simply liked and admired him, and that was all. Wasn't it? She could hardly be falling in love again! Not so soon after a traumatic bust-up with a fiancé—well, almost-fiancé—of six long months. And not with a man she barely knew, either. No, she decided firmly, she was not infatuated with Alex St Cloud. And she was not going to be, either.

The faint hum of the petrol line had stopped, and she could hear the clanking of the reinforcing chain as the mechanics uncoupled the long hose from the yacht's side.

She stood up as Alex came in to the wheelhouse.

'Let's get out of this stinking harbour,' he said shortly, and she nodded. For the first time, *Mistral*'s twin engines began to throb, a deep note that rose above the clamour and bustle of the harbour. Alex steered the yacht carefully through the myriad boats that cluttered the oily waters of the harbour, and soon *Mistral* was crossing the turbulent waves at the mouth of the breakwater. The noises and smells of Djibouti faded behind them. They hoisted the yacht's tall black-and-white sails, and the warm breeze drove them onwards into the Red Sea. Within an hour they had passed the straits at Bab el Mandeb, and had entered the wide, calm darkness of the Red Sea itself. The moon was full to-night, a great golden disc in the sky above, and in the still, warm darkness the stars sparkled like jewels. Alex cut the engines, and the full-bellied sails drove *Mistral* silently on.

Once again, activity on the yacht tailed off. They were alone on the wide, dark sea, and once Alex had set the automatic pilot, there was little to do. The instruments were still lying on the chart table, where she had been polishing them, and Nicolette picked them to replace them in their cases. The sextant, a heavy, triangular apparatus, slipped through her fingers, and to her horror, hit the deck with a crack. She snatched it up anxiously. The little crystal lens was smashed, and her heart sank. The instrument was a beautiful, obviously antique and much-loved thing. She was peering at it dismally as Alex came in.

'What was that noise?' he asked, then saw the sextant in her hand. She handed it to him guiltily, and he looked at the broken instrument.

'My father gave me this,' he said quietly, and looked up at her with arctic eyes. 'It was his grandfather's.'

'I'm sorry, Alex—'

'Isn't there anything you can do right?' he asked bitterly.

Her nerves taut, Nicolette met his gaze fiercely. 'It was an accident,' she said tensely. 'Can't you believe that? People do have accidents, Alex. I didn't mean to break it—'

'You didn't mean anything, did you?' he said brutally, his own resentments and frustrations rising to breaking point. 'Everything that happens to you happens by accident, doesn't it? It's never your own damned stupid fault, is it?'

'Who the blazes do you think you are,' she retorted with shrill anger, 'some kind of infallible god? You've done nothing but snap and snarl at me ever since you met me—as though I was responsible for all your bad luck!' She turned away, shaking with anger. 'I've done my best to help you, Alex, though I'll never know why. I don't know why I didn't let you take me back to Mombasa that morning—'

'I don't know why I didn't,' he snapped, his wide eyes sparkling with temper. 'I don't need you, Nicolette—you thrust yourself upon me uninvited—'

'Then you can put me ashore at Port Said,' she answered in a trembling voice, 'and I'll find my own way back to England!'

'Port Said!' he jeered. 'How the hell will you find your way out of Port Said?'

'I—I don't know. But—'

'You haven't got a penny, have you?' he taunted.

'I—' She hesitated, flushing.

'You're just supercargo, Nicolette,' he told her savagely.

She spun round, her eyes bright with unshed tears, and made for the door of the wheelhouse. His hand caught her wrist in a vicelike grip, and he jerked her ruthlessly around to face him. She gasped, staring up into the intent, bearded face above her.

'Let me go, damn you!' she hissed. Her wrist was hurting.

'Why?' he asked with deceptive softness. 'It's the way men treat their concubines, isn't it?'

'What do you mean?'

'Seeing that you've told the world you're my mistress, little Nicolette, we might as well make the most of it.' Alex pulled her close to him, his magnificent grey eyes intent.

'I don't know what you're talking about,' she faltered nervously, trying to pull away.

'Poor little innocent,' he said silkily. 'Let me show you.' He lifted her chin with a strong hand, and kissed her full on the lips. He was still wearing only his shorts, and his naked skin was cool against her warm flesh. She froze in shock, then thrust away, her hands pressing on the hard muscles of his chest and ribs.

'Let me go!'

'I'm beginning to think you may have your uses after all,' Alex purred, his eyes thoughtful, smouldering. Her lips carried the memory of his firm mouth, the bristle of his beard. She stared at him, transfixed, knowing that he was going to kiss her again, but unable to resist. His arms pulled her closer against his tall, hard body as his mouth took hers again. Suddenly panicking, she tried to struggle free, but he was incredibly strong, his arms pinioning hers. Her little yelp of alarm was lost as his mouth thrust with ruthless power against her lips, forcing them apart, pressing hard against her tightly-clenched teeth. She could feel his chest-muscles hard against her, and when she tried to twist her head away, his hand came up, and he ran strong fingers through her cropped hair, twisting the short golden curls so that she could not move. Then her lips parted, and his warm lips moved against hers, forcing her to respond. And a deep, irresistible warmth had begun to spread through her stomach, slackening the tense muscles like the fingers of an expert masseur, so that she felt herself melting against him, her hips drifting against his with shuddering delight. Her mouth melted in surrender too, and as his lips caressed hers roughly, she answered him, slowly at first, and then with mounting passion, as his kiss became deeper and stronger, possessing her as no man had ever possessed her. When at last he released her, she almost fell, and he caught her limp body with quick hands, lowering her on to the leather-backed settee where she had been sitting. Their eyes met.

'So,' he said, his voice slightly rough. 'Now we know.' Her mouth felt bruised, numb; she raised a shaking hand to touch it.

'Wh-what do you mean?' she whispered.

'Now we know why you told all those stories,' he said, his beautiful eyes intent, amused. 'You want to be in my bed, don't you?'

'No!'

'No?' He sat beside her with an ironic smile, and thrust her back, so that she fell into his arms, and found herself looking into the intoxicating wildness of his face. 'Shall we retire to the civilised comforts of my cabin? Or should we simply do it right here?'

'Neither!' she yelped, seriously frightened. 'I don't want to go to bed with you!'

'Your mouth tells me otherwise,' Alex said drily. 'No woman kisses like that who doesn't mean it, Nicolette Mercury.' The golden light of the hurricane lamp was casting soft highlights on the sleek muscles of his arms and shoulders; the rest of his body was in a bronze shadow.

'I—I—just because you've kissed me it doesn't mean you've got the right to force me into bed with you,' she said breathlessly.

'I'm not going to force you anywhere,' he said, his deep voice deceptively calm and gentle. His hand came up to brush her short curls back, his eyes amused, supremely confident.

'This mad haircut isn't altogether unattractive,' he growled, as she stared up at him, hypnotised by the movement of his fingers through her hair. His fingers ran through the glinting curls with smooth, bone-melting strokes, and like a cat, Nicolette began to arch her neck against the intoxicating pleasure of the sensation. His laugh was deep, mocking, and then his fingers tugged at her hair hard enough to make her gasp with pain, and his mouth was over hers. And this time, she could not even pretend to resist. His lips explored her mouth with a deliberate awareness, an arrogant pleasure, that made her senses swim. She found that her fingers were digging into the hard, springy muscles of his neck, shakily caressing his thick hair. His hand slid under her shirt, making her shudder, and deftly unhooked the top of her bikini. As his palm brushed with careless possessiveness over her taut breasts, she cried out, low and soft, and twisted out of his arms with a final effort that left her spent and gasping on her feet. She leaned against the chart table as he straightened, and looked at her with cynical, damnably attractive eyes.

'What now?' he asked sardonically. 'More tricks?'

'I—I don't want to go on with this, Alex.'

'Oh yes, you do,' Alex said coolly. 'Look at your hands, my dear Nicolette—you're trembling like a leaf!'

'I just don't happen to be available,' she said, her voice husky in her throat. 'Not like this, anyway.'

'How, then? Do you have to be wooed and tempted? I'm afraid the Red Sea is rather short on roses,' he sneered.

'I'm not available at all,' she said, winning a little control over her rebellious body. She met his eyes, her face reddening. 'Is this your idea of punishment, Alex? Do you want to humiliate me, because you don't like me—because I've been a minor irritation?'

'Nonsense,' he said calmly. 'This has nothing to do with anything except our bodies. I'm a man, you're a woman. We both want sex. What else enters into it?'

'A hell of a lot enters into it,' she snapped. 'For one thing, I don't want sex. I'm not that sort of girl.'

'What sort are you, then?' he retorted. 'The sort who tells her fiancé that she's sleeping with another man? The sort who steals her way into someone else's life? What kind of girl is that, Nicolette?'

'A confused girl, maybe,' she said quietly. 'But not the sort of girl who jumps into every stranger's bed.'

'Oh, come,' he laughed, standing up and coming towards her, 'spare me the virginal innocence!'

'Don't!' she said sharply, stepping hastily out of the door. In the warm darkness on the deck, his arms found her, pulling her close against his body, so close that she could feel how much he wanted her. The blood rushed to her face. He was so very strong that he could have forced his way with her in seconds.

'Alex,' she begged desperately, 'please let me go!' Something of the urgency in her tone communicated itself to him. Silently he released her, and she stepped back weakly, a horrible pang of disappointment washing through her. With heightened instincts, she could feel that he had suddenly become cold.

'Nicolette,' he rasped, his voice like steel, 'let me give you one warning—don't play with me. Ever. Understood?'

'Yes,' she whispered. He turned, and strode angrily into the warm night. A miserable, shaking reaction was setting in, and Nicolette clasped her arms around herself, feeling the unsatisfied ache spreading through her body, an empty pain that she knew Alex could have taken from her in seconds, replacing it with—

So—she had saved her precious honour. And that was good. Wasn't it?

CHAPTER FIVE

NICOLETTE was awake in the pink dawn, lying restlessly on her bunk. Through the porthole the early morning sun sent a shaft of clear light to splash across her naked upper body. She thrust the sheets away, already feeling hot. She had slept badly, her dreams confused and alarmingly delicious, dreams in which Alex's face had appeared with remarkable frequency.

She rose, clad only in her panties, and went to the porthole to look out, hugging her breasts. The flat sea was a rose-tinted silver, as calm and peaceful as an English millpond. *Mistral* was sailing smoothly up the Red Sea like a great grey albatross drifting on high winds. All was quiet. Nicolette pulled on her bikini, splashed her face with water, and contemplated her reflection ruefully in the glass. The golden mop was growing with maddening slowness. She recalled Alex's fingers through it last night with a shock of memory, and saw the change in her own brown eyes. What was happening to her? Thinking of her own reactions last night, pressed against the exciting strength of Alex's body, she felt a hot wave of shame pass through her. Dear heaven! She had been almost out of control, unable to stop herself from responding to his expert caresses.

Unable to meet her own accusing brown eyes, she turned and went quietly up on to the deck to bathe her near-naked body in the last cool breezes of the dawn. The sun was already a flaming ball rising out of the long, thin line to the East, the line she knew was Saudi Arabia. She sighed, leaning over the rail at *Mistral*'s beautiful, elegant prow, and stared down into the glassy, rushing water that creamed delicately around her bows. Yesterday had been quite a day. Mark's voice, issuing from the radio set, had shaken her more than she cared to admit. The cool indifference in his tone had brought it home to her—more forcefully than anything else could have done—that things between them had finally come to a conclusion. She recalled that horrible telephone conversation in Momba-sa, the sick shock that had filled her as he told her about Geraldine—Geraldine, whose almond eyes had always watched her with a sly amusement she had never been able to fathom. Well, now she knew the cause of the older girl's quiet smiles. No doubt she had been amusing the others for weeks with the story—how Nicolette was too proper, too 'middle-class' to sleep with Mark Macmillan. How he had found his pleasure elsewhere.

Could Mark really believe that she was having an affair with Alex St Cloud? It came to her in a flash that he didn't. Of course he didn't—but it was the perfect opportunity for him to cut the last remaining ties with her. Mark would probably have felt bound by the chivalrous conventions of his upper-class background. No matter how bored he became with her, he would not be able to simply cast her off. And she had neatly provided him with the classic reason for breaking off their engagement.

And she realised, with a hardening of her heart, that there had been unmistakable relief in his voice as he had informed her in Mombasa, with the precision of a stockbroker, that things were now at an end between them. In fact, she now could see clearly how Mark had set the whole revelation up. She had not wormed the truth out of him—he had wanted her to know, had forced the subject into the conversation. He had *wanted* to end their engagement, their almost-but-not-quite engagement.

She rubbed the brass rail absently, trying to locate some area of pain in her heart. She should by rights have been shattered by the turn events had taken. Yet she was not. Had she become cynical?

And what about Alex St Cloud? Had he already breached her defences, taken possession of her heart? How could there be possession when all he wanted from her was sex—earthy and powerful, unrefined by any complications? Such as love? Or even tenderness? The sun spread warm fingers across her body, and she turned to look back the way they had come. The sea was deserted and calm, a sheet of liquid gold where the sun lit it. Nicolette glanced down at her own long legs. She had always been blessed with a good figure, slender and delicately made, her breasts uptilted and full. The sun of the past few days had gilded her skin, turning it the rich, fine tint of ripening wheat. The violet bikini set her skin off perfectly, and she wondered almost idly how Alex saw her.

Did her body arouse him? The thought made the fine hairs on her arms rise with a little prickle. He had made it clear last night that he wanted her. She remembered the pressure of his body in the darkness and shook the voluptuous thought away angrily. He would probably have behaved in the same way if she had been hideous, or a withered old crone. There was no flattery to be found in the thought that he had wanted to make love to her. No,

she corrected herself, had wanted to—the words that rose
to her mind were too ugly to think. Have sex with her,
then. He was a mature man. That magnificent body, so
packed with hard male power, would naturally have its
desires and needs. Like eating. Or sex. And she had been
convenient—available. That was all. Above all, she must
not be lured into any sentimental notions about Alex—
that would be fatal. He would rip her heart to ribbons if
she ever allowed him to take it in his grasp. He was not the
loving kind. Not for little Nicolette Mercury, a twenty-
three-year-old innocent abroad. Yet how easily he had
melted her last night, how very easily! And how exquisite
it would have been to have surrendered to him, to have let
him take her, body and soul, and to let him transport her
to the ecstasy she had glimpsed in his kisses. A fragment of
poetry spun into her head, making her shudder—something about a woman wailing for her demon lover. She
looked up into the clear blue sky, wondering about Alex St
Cloud.

'Sun-worshipping?' She turned to see him coming out of
the wheelhouse door, a splendid bronze figure towelling
his face dry. Then he dropped the towel, and she gasped.
He had shaved off his beard.

'It's going to be too hot for a beard over the next few
days,' he said casually. She gaped at him. He had left
short sideburns, but his face was naked—a shockingly
beautiful face! With a bold, square chin and a mouth that
smiled mockingly, deliciously, at her amazement.

'You—you're beautiful!' she gasped, unembarrassed
by her own words. He turned away with a faint smile, and
she stared at the firm, strong curve of his jawline; it was a
face that matched the classical perfection of his body to

the full, an utterly male face that carried no spare flesh. The mouth was sensuous, a mouth made to make women shudder; and his straight Norman nose and level eyes gave a severe calm to what might otherwise have been the face of a rake, a buccaneer who dined off women as a gourmet dines off pheasants and grouse.

Do you have much of that sort of trouble, Mr St Cloud? It's been known to crop up.

The words of that conversation rose unbidden in her mind.

'Please don't stand with your mouth open,' said Alex sardonically. 'I'm sure I'm not that stunning—flattering though your attention is.'

She tore her eyes away from him, and tried to match the coolness in his voice.

'No, you aren't that stunning after all. Would you like some breakfast?'

'Yes,' he said, unmoved by her sarcasm. 'First let's put some more canvas up—I want to take advantage of any wind there might be.' He stepped down to one of the lockers, and hauled out a genoa. They raised the extra sail, and *Mistral* responded with an added thrust into the limpid water. Yet Nicolette could not keep her eyes off him. That shaggy beard had concealed one of the most marvellous male faces she had ever seen, and she wondered why on earth he had ever grown it. To cover a face like that argued a certain lack of vanity. But Alex was not vain. Arrogant, yes, proud of his strength and his fitness, proud the way a mettled race-horse might be—but not vain. Not vain in the way Mark had been vain about his almost girlish good looks. How vague and shadowy Mark seemed in comparison to this man!

Over breakfast, they were silent, neither of them referring to the night before.

'How long will it take us to get into the Mediterranean?' asked Nicolette. He shrugged.

'That depends on the wind. And other things. But about twenty-four hours now.'

'As little as that?'

'If the wind holds. We're making excellent time.' He dabbed at the remains of his egg with a piece of bread, swallowed it, and looked at her with level grey eyes.

'Mercury,' he said. 'Where does the name come from?'

'My great-grandfather,' she said with a smile. 'He was a Greek, a raisin-merchant. His name was Costas Mercouri. But no one could spell it, so it gradually changed to Mercury.'

He glanced at her hair and the golden skin of her throat. 'You don't look very Greek to me,' he commented.

'No,' she admitted. 'Costas had hair as black as pitch, but all my grandparents had fair hair.'

'Your mother?'

'Her hair was the same colour as mine. Or so my father told me.'

There was a pause, while Alex looked searchingly into her eyes. 'Mmmm. Perhaps your children will turn out black-haired and olive-skinned.'

'Perhaps,' she said, embarrassed by his mention of her children. 'St Cloud's an unusual name. Where does it originate?'

'It's a corruption of Saint Claude,' he said. 'From a town in Provence.'

'I suppose your family came over with the Conqueror,' she said lightly.

'They came over on the Dover-Calais ferry,' he told her drily. 'At least, my father did. He's a Frenchman through and through.'

'Really?' she said, intrigued. 'And your mother?'

'She was English. She and my father met during the war—he was in the Resistance, based in Toulon, and when he had to leave in a hurry to get away from the Nazis, he came to London. They met, and fell in love. After the war was over, he came back to England to marry her.'

'Julian said he's one of the best boat-designers in Europe,' she prompted.

A rare smile crossed Alex's firm mouth.

'He'd be delighted to hear that,' he said. 'He's always been twenty years ahead of his time. It's generally taken that long for his ideas to be accepted. Anyway, now that he's in his sixties, his genius is beginning to be recognised.' He gestured at *Mistral*'s smooth white decks.

'And you design executive jets for the super-rich,' she said, a hint of mischief in her eyes.

He nodded.

'Yes. For some reason I was more drawn to the air than to the sea. Three years ago I floated a company—Cloud Aerospace. It cost a fortune, and we're just paying off our debts now. But next year—and if the Germans buy one of my helicopter designs for their traffic police, we should be in business. And you, Miss Mercouri—are you one of the idle rich?'

She explained about her restoration work, and to her surprise he was interested. 'I didn't think that sort of thing would mean much to you,' she said.

'On the contrary—what you're doing is vitally important. The past is precious—and fragile. It has to be preserved, otherwise it simply disintegrates. And then we all lose touch with where we came from. Which makes it all the more difficult to see where we're going. Speaking of which,' he said, rising, 'we'd better cut the chatter. We're going to be coming into the Shaibera Archipelago soon, and there are lots of shoals and shallows to contend with.' His grey eyes met hers with mocking irony. 'Just like life. Don't you think so, little virgin?'

They were among the islands by ten-thirty, a myriad sandy humps and banks rising out of the sea, some covered with rough grass, others with date palms and coconut trees growing on them. The yacht glided between them, Nicolette keeping a careful look-out for shoals. After half an hour, one larger than the rest came into view, a grass-covered hump rising out of the glassy water. To Nicolette's astonishment, a castle seemed to have been built on the summit. She called to Alex, who nodded.

'That's Mar'abi,' he told her.

'Is it a real castle?'

'I don't know,' he shrugged, shading his grey eyes to stare at the island. 'It looks vaguely Moorish. Something left over from the Crusades, perhaps.'

As they sailed closer, Nicolette could see that it was indeed a castle, many of its sand-coloured walls tumbling down, and obviously deserted. The battlements had been crenellated in an unmistakably Moorish design. It was an eerie, haunting place. On impulse, she turned to Alex, who had come to stare up at it with her.

'Can we stop, Alex? Just to have a look at it?'

He glanced at her ironically. 'This is not a pleasure

cruise, Nicolette.' He looked at his watch. 'But we're making good time. All right, let's take a look.'

There was a small natural bay to one side of the island, and they anchored *Mistral* as shallow as they dared, and swam ashore in the warm water. It was a short, steep climb to the castle, and to her pleasure Nicolette saw that the grass was full of purple and red poppies, nodding in the slight breeze. The walls of the ruin rose high above them as they walked through the huge gateway that in ancient times would have been so stoutly defended.

The roofless interior of the castle was a wilderness of poppies and coarse grass. It was as calm and still as a tomb, only the wind sighing gently through the ruined battlements and among the swaying poppies. They walked in silence through the huge halls, listening to the mysterious music of the wind. There was a crumbling flight of steps against one of the sturdier walls, and they climbed gingerly to the top, and sat together on the battlement, gazing around them. *Mistral* was a beautiful grey shape in the blue bay below them, casting a gull's-wing reflection in the clear water. The Red Sea was calm and deserted around them, stretching like a vast lake to the horizon, where the coast of Egypt was visible as a faint smudge. The islands of the Archipelago were scattered around them like tawny gems on watered silk.

'It's beautiful!' she breathed.

Alex nodded, tossing a stone over the edge of the parapet.

'Yes. This place must have been built by the Moors to keep a watch out for Crusaders.'

'How old do you think it is?'

'Seven, eight hundred years. It's a strange place. "As

holy and enchanted as e'er beneath a waning moon was haunted by woman wailing for her demon lover".' He smiled at her with mocking eyes, and she started.

'I was trying to remember that poem this morning,' she said. 'What is it?'

'Coleridge—*Kubla Khan*. Come on, let's get back to the boat. We've a long way to go.'

She followed him down, still entranced by the lonely, wild beauty of Mar'abi. As they walked through the poppies, Alex suddenly stooped, and picked something up. It was a hoop of some metal, covered in earth. He rubbed it clean on the rough grass, and examined it. It was a bangle, a thick silver bangle. Nicolette came over with an exclamation of delight.

'Alex, how lovely! What is it?'

'It's a slave bracelet, I think,' he said, studying the design on it. 'It's probably as old as this castle—if not older.' She watched his magnificent face as he turned the thing in his fingers. It was a heavy, solid silver hoop, its worn outlines beautifully chased with Arabic designs. Because of the purity of the metal, it had not tarnished over the centuries, the way modern silver would have done, and the clasp clicked open under the pressure of Alex's fingers.

'It's exquisitely made, isn't it?' she marvelled.

'Yes—some local war-lord would have had this made for his favourite slave-girl.' He showed her the clasp with a dry smile. 'There would have been a little silver lock on it—just to make sure she couldn't take it off and sell it.'

'What a beautiful thing it is! Would someone really have had that made for a common slave-girl?'

A sardonic quirk tugged at the corner of that splendid

mouth. 'You're very innocent sometimes, Nicolette. I wonder whether you really are innocent—or whether you're just a good actress?'

'Oh,' she said. 'You mean she would have been—'

'A favourite concubine. Yes. This would have been a reward for—er—services well rendered.'

'Oh,' she said, looking at the beautiful thing with new eyes. Alex reached over and took her hand. With an unfathomable smile, he clipped the hoop over her wrist. She stared at it in disbelief.

'It's yours,' he said ironically. Nicolette gaped, and then ran after him as he turned and walked briskly down the hillside to the bay where *Mistral* lay waiting.

'Alex, this is probably priceless! You can't just give it away—'

'Why? Are you afraid I'll turn you into my slave-girl?' he retorted drily. 'Come on, let's get back to the boat.' They swam through the deliciously warm water to the yacht, and hauled themselves aboard. The silver bangle was heavy on her wrist, a new, weighty presence on her body. She looked at it in delight—it would polish up to a beautiful sheen, she knew. As they padded across the deck, slippery and wet, Alex stooped to haul up the anchor chain, and she joined him, pulling the lock on the winch free as he wound the chain up. He turned to her, his eyes dropping to her golden figure, clad only in her violet bikini, and then meeting hers with a glint of smoky fire.

Something quivered in Nicolette's stomach, a hard tug of passion that made her gasp silently. He took her quickly in his arms, their wet bodies meeting, thighs touching. She tried to shake her head, but Alex's mouth had found hers—and now the kiss was not the ruthless affair of last night, but a clinging, deliberately sensual caress that set her blood racing. His lips touched hers, first gently, then with a hardening desire that made her bones melt.

'No,' she whispered, her legs weak.

'You mean yes,' he said, his voice mocking as he bent to kiss the side of her neck, his lips tasting the salt water on her smooth, warm skin. She groaned, trying to fight the passion that was welling up in her, and twisted away from his mouth, struggling free of his arms.

'Please, Alex—I told you last night—'

His mouth silenced hers, and then he picked her up in his arms as lightly as though she had been a feather, and carried her into the wheelhouse, laying her down on the settee there. She looked up giddily into his eyes as he settled next to her.

'Alex, don't do this to me!'

His kiss was deep, endlessly thrilling; it was as though his whole being was exploring hers, the hard hands and sensuous lips provoking her, challenging her, until she could bear it no longer, and her body arched up against his, her arms creeping round his neck. Alex's sharp teeth were ruthless against her lips, and she was aware of the faint, musky smell of his skin as the water dripped from their bodies. Afterwards, she looked up at him, panting, her cheeks flushed. His eyes were cool, the desire in them banked down, and his smile was quietly triumphant.

'Don't do what to you, Nicolette? What you want me to do?'

'It's *not* what I want,' she denied, knowing that he would be able to read the lie naked in her face.

'Isn't it? Your eyes tell me different.' His hands moved down her body in a slow, lingering caress, brushing the sides of her breasts, her flanks, the rounded curves of her hips. Nicolette closed her eyes desperately, knowing that the message in them would be all too clear.

'Please stop,' she said through gritted teeth. 'This isn't very gentlemanly, Alex.'

'Who said I was a gentleman?' he purred, his hands repeating the caress with maddening slowness. It was as though a fire had spread through her veins, melting every sinew, every bone in her body. It was all she could do to stop from moaning out, and she grasped his wrists in her own hands to stop him.

'I'm getting up,' she declared shakily, trying to raise herself.

'I see,' he said ironically. 'We're playing the innocent virgin again, are we? You don't have to pretend, Nicolette.'

'I'm not pretending,' she whispered, as his fingers trailed like fire across the thin material of her bikini bottom and across the tops of her thighs. 'I've told you, Alex—I'm not available!'

'No?' The caress was infinitely arousing, infinitely possessive. He bent to kiss her softly in the hollow of her throat, and then again at the side of her neck. She rolled her head to one side with a choking sigh as the kisses reached her ears, his warm breath stirring her curls.

'Is this how you seduce all your women?' she said with bittersweet anger, her mind beginning to dissolve into delicious chaos.

'Don't be so inquisitive,' he reproved her. His tongue drew a line of fire along her lower lip, from one corner of her mouth to the other, and she parted her lips with desperate resolve to tell him no. The words were smothered in a kiss as unashamedly erotic as the act of love itself. For long minutes she was lost in a new world— Alex's world—where her mind was filled with brilliant, soft colours that she had never dreamed of before. Mark's kisses had never been like this! The touch that had seemed so expert to her a few weeks ago was a fumbling boy's caress compared to this utterly masculine, utterly domi-nant power. His confidence was so supreme that he needed to use only the gentlest touch to set her aflame.

She looked up at him through dewy eyes as he smiled mockingly down at her, his deep slate-grey eyes trium-phant.

'It's just a game to you,' she said with trembling anger. 'Isn't it? You just don't care! All you want is my body—'

'What else have you got to offer?' he smiled ironically.

'I'm not offering anything,' she gasped. 'Let me up, Alex—I've had enough of this!'

'We haven't even started,' he said calmly, pushing her firmly back. 'Let's not play games, Nicolette. I've told you once already—don't play with me.'

'I'm not,' she said bitterly. 'It's you who are playing with *me*! Do you think I'm some sort of challenge to be overcome?'

'Any challenge you ever presented has long since been overcome,' he mocked, his beautiful face amused. He slipped off the top of her bikini with a gentle tug, and she panted desperately as his hands covered her breasts, her nipples thrusting into his palms, giving him their own message of desire and acceptance.

'Damn you,' she said, her voice throbbing as she twisted out of his embrace and yanked her costume back into place. She walked away from him on shaky legs, and

then turned to him, the tears she could no longer suppress glistening in her eyes. 'Damn you to hell, Alex St
Cloud!'

He stared at her, one eyebrow rising in urbane astonishment.

'I think you really mean it,' he said softly. Nicolette
turned and walked blindly out into the baking heat of the
deck, and stumbled against the taffrail, a sob of frustration
and shame rising in her throat. She gazed miserably
across the sea, the tears in her eyes breaking the calm
water into a billion dancing turquoises. She fastened her
bikini top with trembling fingers, and brushed the wet off
her cheeks with her wrists. Alex was leaning against the
rail with folded arms, staring out to sea with impassive
grey eyes. She brushed her short curls back with her
hands, wishing she were dead. There was a silence,
broken only by the murmur of the wind in *Mistral*'s steel
rigging. She leaned forward on the polished brass rail.
The heavy silver bangle slipped down her arm and thudded gently against her wrist, and she stared at it dismally,
her stomach and throat aching with misery and unsatisfied longing.

'You really do mean it,' he said quietly. She did not
answer, staring up at the ruined castle of Mar'abi with
tragic brown eyes. Alex turned to her.

'You're a virgin, aren't you?' he asked. She tensed, then
nodded her head fractionally. He sighed, with a mixture of
anger and impatience on his face.

'You could have told me that a long time ago, Nicolette,
and saved us both a lot of bother.'

'It's not the sort of thing people just say to one another,'
she said tiredly. 'Just because you've given me this slave-

bracelet it doesn't mean that I automatically become your slave, Alex.'

'Nicolette—' For the first time, she saw him hesitate. 'You must admit that the way you came on board this yacht was calculated to make me think that—' He paused.

'That I was chasing you?' she suggested bitterly. 'That I was waiting to be seduced?'

'Something like that,' he admitted quietly. 'Nice girls don't chop off all their hair to bluff their way on to a yacht with a strange man. The sort of girl who behaves like that, Nicolette, only has one thing on her mind.'

'Well, I didn't,' she retorted, her body still shaking.

'No? Then tell me—what *did* you have on your mind?' She met his splendid grey eyes with confusion, and for a long moment they stared at one another. Then Alex shrugged. 'It doesn't matter, does it?' He turned and reached for the guy-ropes to haul up the big mainsail. Nicolette stood silent in the stern, his question echoing through her mind again and again.

By late afternoon, the great grey bluff of the Sinai Peninsula was looming ahead of them. It had been a blazingly hot day. When the heat had become intolerable, they had hosed one another down with the pump, silently and without smiles. She had watched the water spraying from his hard-muscled body and had tried to think of nothing. But now, as the Arabian twilight settled around them, she began to realise that she was confused.

More confused than she had ever been, even during those dark days after her father's death.

Alex's question kept ringing through her head. Why *had* she behaved so madly? She had never in her life behaved with such reckless abandon. Okay, she had been bitterly upset by the telephone call to Mark. And she had been ashamed of her part in the collision in Mombasa. And she had wanted to repay Alex for saving her that day in Serengeti. But were those adequate reasons for what she had done?

It was becoming increasingly difficult for her to think straight about Alex. Not least, she knew, because of what had happened between them last night and this afternoon. That he affected her powerfully was beyond doubt. He exerted a sexual attraction over her that had already almost torn her from her foothold twice. That Alex knew how to make love to a woman was bone-meltingly obvious. Compared to him, Mark's kisses had been fumbling pecks, his hands greedy and cruel. But what else was there in her feelings for Alex?

All he felt for her was sexual desire, she knew that. And it was not something she could respond to; her upbringing, her private code of what was right, prevented her. She had been kissed by men, certainly, and had wondered healthily about sex. Yet she had passed her twenty-second birthday without ever having gone further than the quick kisses and caresses that she had exchanged with Mark Macmillan. She wanted to think about Alex, to sort out her feelings for him—but it was so difficult. There was so much mixed up in her attitude to him—the dislike she had felt for his autocratic behaviour, the respect for his self-control and power, the scalding desire that had spilled through her veins when he had touched her breasts with those strong brown hands . . .

They were close enough to land to smell it now, a heady fragrance of aloes and myrrh that the warm wind carried from Sinai across the sea. The dusk was violet and purple, and cool enough for a T-shirt and a pair of denim shorts. The wind was against them, and Alex had started *Mistral*'s engines. Their deep throb was comforting, almost maternal, under her feet. With a sigh, she went to the galley to make something to eat. She peered into the icy, smoking depths of the freezer, and settled on lamb chops and a few assorted vegetables.

Alex was using the big radio set as she brought the meal in, the headphones round his ears. He nodded his thanks as she put the plate down, and listened intently, making notes on a pad in front of him. At length, he took the headset off, and tucked into his meal.

'That was the weather report,' he said. 'There's a big depression moving over the Mediterranean now.'

'Is that bad news?' she asked as they ate.

'No, it's good news for the time being. But it may mean some dirty weather in a few days. With luck we'll be well away before it arrives.' They ate in silence. He looked at her with calm grey eyes as he pushed his plate away. 'We'll be in the Gulf of Suez in half an hour,' he told her. 'In the Mediterranean by to-morrow afternoon, if all goes well.' He rose, a tall, powerful figure in his light cotton shirt. 'Let's go on to the bridge and watch Suez come up.'

They stood in the mild air on the bridge, gazing at the rocky peninsula of Sinai pass by on their starboard side. The sun had already set, leaving a crimson and purple wash in the sky that darkened to a deep blue overhead, revealing the first stars.

'Tell me about your father,' said Alex unexpectedly. She turned to look at him, but his face was turned ahead, his eyes watching the darkening sky ahead.

'Well,' she began hesitantly, 'he was a big man. He always wore a beard—I never saw him without one. Dad was an architect. Not a very successful one, I'm afraid. I think he was really a sailor at heart, but he had to conform to what his family expected of him.'

'Go on.'

'He loved the sea. He was out every weekend on the sloop. It was called *Nicolette*,' she added with a little smile. 'He designed schools, hospitals, that sort of thing. But there never seemed to be enough work. Maybe he just didn't try hard enough. He was content if we had enough to live on—and to keep the boat equipped.'

'You used to go out with him?'

'Yes, often. He loved sailing alone, but I would go with him whenever I could. In my school holidays we went everywhere—Norway, Denmark, France. The furthest we went was Italy, one summer.'

'But you weren't with him on his last voyage?' Alex asked quietly, turning to her. She shook her head, remembering those terrible days.

'No. He went out on a Friday afternoon. By Sunday there was no word of him, and there was a big gale blowing. I had to wait until the next Friday before they found the boat. And even then they kept on looking.'

'I'm sorry,' he said gently.

'It's past now,' she said, with another little smile.

'How old were you?' he asked, looking at her, his eyes flicking to her cropped blonde hair.

'Sixteen.'

There was a silence. In the gathering dusk, *Mistral* steamed past a white-sailed dhow. The man at the tiller was singing, a sweet, strange, plaintive folk tune that was thousands of years old. The haunting voice floated over the water to them, the voice of Arabia—patient, resigned, melancholy. As the song drifted behind them, Alex reached for her with astonishingly tender arms, pulling her backwards so that she was resting against him, her head cradled against his chest. She lay in his arms passively, her eyes dim. His lips brushed her hair gently.

'How did you cope?' he said in a low voice.

'Badly,' she confessed. 'I was dry-eyed for weeks, and then it suddenly hit me that I was really never going to see him again. Then I cried for days. I didn't even have a grave to mourn over. And then I realised that the sea was his grave—his monument.'

'Yes,' he said gently. 'And your mother?'

'All I ever knew of her was a marble gravestone in Highgate Cemetery,' she said. 'It's all a bit maudlin, isn't it?' She laughed, a little sound that wasn't far off a sob. His arms were warm and strong around her, his broad chest a pillow for all her aches and confusion. How blissful it would be to sleep in his arms to-night—to forget everything but this big man and the comfort he could give her, lost in the eternal closeness of his body. The gentle dusk was changing imperceptibly into night. *Mistral* was in the Gulf of Suez now, and the pungent smells of the land were blowing across her decks—smells of campfires, of strange, alien households, whose roofs were the stars. Out there, in the warm twilight, nightingales would be singing. Other men would be holding other women, other lives would be meeting, intersecting, parting . . .

There was a feeling in her heart that she had never known before, a yearning that was filling her entire being.

'Alex,' she said inconsequentially, 'you're not married,

are you?' After a pause, he released her, and she turned to face him. In the soft dusk she could see that his eyes were clear and cold.

'Listen, Nicolette,' he said in a cool voice, 'I told you not to have any romantic fantasies about me, didn't I?'

'Yes,' she whispered, taken aback by his tone.

'I meant it, Nicolette. Don't get involved with me. As for your question—no, I've never been married. Satisfied?'

'Yes,' she whispered again.

'Good. We're going to have to take watches at night from now on—the area is full of small boats, and I don't want to hit anything else before we get back to England. You'll take the early morning watch—from three till seven. So if I were you, I'd turn in now. Got that?'

'Yes,' she said again.

'I'll wake you at three. Goodnight, Nicolette.'

'Goodnight,' she said quietly. He walked up to the mast, and raised *Mistral*'s riding lights. She took the plates from the wheelhouse, washed them in the galley, and then flopped down on her bunk, feeling drained.

But it was a long time before she slept.

CHAPTER SIX

THE Suez Canal was hot, dull—and interminable. Nicolette sat tiredly in the shade of the wheelhouse, watching the flat desert countryside pass by, just visible over the grey concrete walls of the canal. They had passed through the Great Bitter Lake earlier that morning, while she had been sleeping off the weariness left by her early morning watch, and she had woken to find that *Mistral* was already in the long, roofless tunnel of the Canal. She was reminded of rats in a maze as she glanced back to see the long procession of boats and ships behind them.

On the banks of the canal, teams of skinny oxen dragged wooden ploughs over muddy fields, already baking in the noonday sun, and here and there teams of men were digging irrigation ditches, bringing that most precious commodity of all—fresh water—to the fields.

Her dream of seeing the Pyramids was going to stay unfulfilled, she realised. She stared at the flat hills, and wondered what was going through Alex's mind. He had reacted so fiercely to her innocent question about his marital status—why? Had something happened to him, something to embitter him against women? That, at least, would explain his ruthless, almost bitter attitude towards sex. The way in which he was prepared to use her, simply to slake his bodily need for passion, had disturbed Nicolette. Had someone hurt him, some woman who had been cruel or foolish, so that he now saw sex as merely an animal hunger, like any other hunger?

It was dawning on Nicolette that she knew incredibly little about Alex. That he ran an aircraft design firm. That his mother was dead. That his father was French. What else? That he was the most staggeringly attractive man she had ever met? That he disturbed her, thrilled her, excited her, hurt her more bitterly and lastingly than any man she had ever known or dreamed of? It was not enough for her to realise, inevitably, that Alex was making a place in her soul. Nicolette had been raised in a hard school; her father's training had taught her early on to know and judge herself carefully, and she was too self-aware not to realise that any couple, thrown together on a long sea voyage alone, would become attracted—even come to feel something like love for one another. Yet such 'shipboard romances' were illusory. In the bustle and noise of the home port, the romance would evaporate and be gone. She needed to know about Alex, needed to find out about him, and be able to settle her feelings properly. Perhaps his cabin would yield some clues. Even a photograph. She resolved to sneak into Alex's cabin next to the chart-room at the earliest opportunity, and see what she could find.

The Canal stretched endlessly ahead of them, baking in the heat. A shimmering current of hot air lay over everything, as though the earth were an open fire. The sky, she realised, was no longer blue, but a dull, heavy grey. The air was muggy, horribly humid and cloying, and there was an unpleasant, waiting atmosphere in the sky. She walked up on to the bridge, wearing only her bikini and a straw hat. The past few days on *Mistral* had removed any surplus fat that her body might have carried, and she was slim, tanned a delicious brown, and feeling very fit. Only her breasts and gently rounded hips gave an air of voluptuousness to her young body. If only her hair would grow a little faster! It was still a strangely short golden mop, and the sun was fast bleaching it to the fiery white of platinum on top, so that it looked like a precious helmet. Yet Alex had said it was 'not unattractive'. She remembered those strong fingers running so gently, so excitingly through her short hair, and felt the familiar dropping feeling in her stomach that she had come to associate with Alex St Cloud.

He was standing on the bridge, watching the Canal ahead through a heavy pair of binoculars.

'It's so muggy,' she complained, 'and the sky is such a horrible colour.'

'Yes,' he said quietly. 'I don't like it. That nasty weather may be closer than the Met. Office predicted.'

'Do you think so?'

'Mmmm. We'll have to pay special attention to the weather report to-night.' He turned to face her, his thrilling grey eyes running quickly up and down her body. '*Mistral* seems to be doing you good,' he commented drily.

'I was just wishing my hair would grow faster,' she said shyly, delighted at his slight praise. He glanced at her, a sardonic smile tugging at that devastating mouth.

'Women are so vain,' he said. 'As a matter of fact, that haircut quite suits you, Nicolette.'

'Do you think so? As a matter of fact, the vainest people I've ever known have been men.'

'Maybe,' he grunted, turning away. 'But not about things like their hair or clothes. I wish we were out of this damned canal and into the Mediterranean. I don't like the idea of facing a heavy storm with only you for crew.'

'What's wrong with me?' she demanded, hurt. 'Haven't I been efficient enough?' He turned back to her, his face amused, and stared at her for a few heart-stopping seconds.

'Yes,' he said at last, 'I guess that wasn't very fair. You've been all right. I didn't mean that the way it sounded.'

'Then you *would* face a storm with me?' she asked, smiling. His face changed, a chill creeping into those magnificent eyes, and he stared at her a few seconds longer. Then he turned back to his charts and shrugged slightly. 'We'll have to see,' he said indifferently. Feeling that she had been dismissed, she stamped angrily off. Why was it that she could never seem to get through his defences? Why was it always she who came off hurt or snubbed from all their encounters? Damn! If only she could affect him in some way—

She hauled the deck-chair from the tiny saloon on to the deck, and slumped into it, wondering whether she would ever be cool again.

By the middle of the afternoon, they were passing through the last hundred yards of the Canal, and into the filthy pool of Port Said. It was hard to believe that the clean blue Mediterranean lay somewhere ahead of this crowded and smoggy port. As they sailed past the huge concrete blocks at the harbour entrance, she and Alex hauled up all the canvas they had, and a brisk wind threw *Mistral* forward into the blue waves. Alex secured the guys, and announced that he was going to check their starboard engine.

'It hasn't been sounding quite happy,' he told her. 'There might be a few teething troubles, and we'd better have them both working perfectly in case of bad weather.'

With a large toolkit in one hand, he clambered down into the engine room at the stern of the yacht, leaving Nicolette to keep a lookout from the deck. The sky was darkening gradually, although the sun was not going to set for at least two hours. She looked up. It was decidedly peculiar weather, she decided, because although it was growing dark, there were no actual clouds to be seen at all. There were none of the heavy piles of cumulus which she knew could bring devastation in the form of thunder and hail, not even the high wisps of white cloud which could signal winds. But there was a heavy haze building up, and the sea, though calm, was gradually changing to a drab grey as the sunlight faded.

She could hear Alex working down in the engines, and she stepped down the companionway to fetch a novel from her cabin. The door to Alex's cabin was ajar. She hesitated for a moment, her heart beginning to beat faster. Alex would be busy for at least an hour yet. Could she abandon her post on the deck for a few minutes? With an uncomfortable feeling that she was spying, she pushed the door noiselessly open, and stepped into Alex's cabin.

She glanced around. It was, as she might have expected, spotlessly neat. Over the tiny desk was a bookshelf, and she stepped over to glance at the handful of books it contained. A strange mixture—one or two manuals of seamanship, *Jane's Ships of the World*, *Ulysses* by James Joyce, a few old copies of *Time* magazine, a few thrillers, an anthology of poetry—she recalled his quotation to her on Mar'abi—some books in French, a thick manual on aerodynamics and wing mechanics. A beautifully-bound leather copy of the *Rubaiyat of Omar Khayyam* caught her eye. She lifted it out, and flipped the title page open.

The inscription, in a woman's elegant handwriting, read simply 'To Alex, with all my love.' There was no signature. A jealous pang shot through her as she replaced the book. Who had sent all her love to Alex?

Under the bookcase was a collection of photographs, and she examined them eagerly. Two or three were of a silver-haired, hawk-faced man she knew would be Alex's father. An older, more faded shot of a beautiful, smiling woman with calm eyes was unmistakably his mother. One or two were of boats. One was of Jacques Cousteau. One was of a scarlet helicopter hovering a few feet off the ground; she peered closer—the smiling pilot was Alex. The person next to him was a woman, with long brown hair and sunglasses, her face turned slightly away. She stared hungrily through the collection, trying to glean information about Alex from it.

The desk itself contained little of any interest—a small portable typewriter, carefully bolted down, a battered biscuit tin. She opened it. It was full of letters. Most were bills and legal documents, certificates of entry and exit from various ports, manifests of fuel and spare parts. There were three dog-eared letters which began *Mon Cher Fils*, and which she did not look at.

And there was a letter which began simply, 'Darling Man . . .' The acid quiver of jealousy shot through her again as she glanced hastily at the ending: 'Your Trudi.' The letter shook slightly in her hands. Did she have the right to read it? Of course not! The turquoise ink was in the same elegant script as the inscription in the poetry book. Hating herself for her curiosity, Nicolette held the letter closer, knowing that if she did not read it now, it would haunt her for ever after. The date was from a few months ago. She had read the first line when to her horror, the door swung open, and Alex walked in, cleaning his hands on a piece of rag. His eyes met hers with cold surprise.

'What are you doing in here?' he demanded, as she snatched the letter behind her back.

'Nothing,' she stammered. 'I was looking for a book to read—'

His eyes dropped to the open tin on the desk, and then met hers again. Now there was deep anger in them.

'What are you hiding behind your back?' he snapped. She shook her head, her mouth dry with fright.

'N-nothing, Alex.'

He held out his hand. 'Give it to me.'

'It's nothing,' she said breathlessly, 'j-just a book—' With angry ease, he spun her around, and pulled the letter out of her hands. As she turned to face him, his eyes were arctic. In a sudden panic, she thought he was going to hit her.

'*Alex*—'

'So you add spying to all your other accomplishments,' he snarled, his face white with anger. 'Damn you, Nicolette! What the hell were you doing, spying into this letter?'

'I—' She closed her mouth. What on earth could she say to justify her actions? *I think I'm falling in love with you, and I need to know more than your name?* 'I—I wanted to find out more about you, Alex, I—'

His face was set with fury, a fury she could not understand. Or was it half-pain? With a sudden chill around the heart, she realised that she had trespassed unforgivably, had blundered into some area of Alex's private life that he had wanted never to think of again.

'I—I'm so sorry,' she faltered.

'You stupid little sneak!' he said, his voice rough with anger. He flicked the letter away, and one brown hand reached for her savagely, tightening in the soft hair at the back of her head, and jerking her close to him, so that she gasped with pain.

'Alex,' she cried, her palms pressing against the hard, tense muscles of his chest, 'I never read that letter, I swear it!'

His eyes were intent on hers, their expression changing from icy fury to something else, something that made her knees turn to jelly and her heart falter. He kissed her, hard and deliberately, until her lips gave way to his, and her hands moved in supplication around his powerful neck. His fingers released their grip in her hair as he let her slip slightly back in his arms. Then, his eyes still holding hers, and a taunting smile curling his cruel mouth, he slowly unfastened the catch at the back of her bikini top, and let the flimsy Lycra garment drop on to the floor. Hypnotised, her heart racing, Nicolette watched his magnificent eyes drop to her breasts.

'God, you're beautiful,' he said softly, and with a little gasp, she found herself in his hard embrace, her breasts pressed to the cool, velvety skin of his ribs, the whole firm length of his body pressed against her. There was an urgency in her now, a need that could not be denied. Shame and morality were evaporating like mist in the sun. She needed him, she needed him so very much that it hurt, ached, tore at her. As he bent to kiss the full swell of her breasts, she whispered his name, her eyes fluttering closed. She felt that she was drifting, her senses swimming in heavy oil. He lifted her on to the bunk, its soft covers cool against her burning skin, and as his mouth found the tips of her aching breasts, she moaned, her hands running through his thick hair.

She opened her eyes slowly to meet his. They contained an expression of triumph, cold and calculating, that chilled her to the bone.

'It doesn't mean a thing to you, does it?' she whispered. 'You don't give a damn for my feelings at all.'

'What point would there be in sentimentalising sex?' he asked brutally. 'It's just a physical contact, nothing more.'

'If you believe that, then I'm sorry for you,' she said bitterly, covering her breasts with her arms, and turning away.

'Are you such an expert on sex?' he mocked, a note of anger in his voice. 'You—a little virgin?'

'Virgin or not,' she snapped, 'I seem to know a lot more about it than you do. Sex isn't just a physical thing—it's the highest expression of the love between two people—'

'The love between two people,' he snarled, his voice rough. 'Don't give me that—I've had all that, Nicolette, as you'd have found out if you'd read that letter!'

'Who is Trudi?' she asked softly. 'Someone you loved?'

'Yes,' he sneered, 'someone I loved—once. Before I found out that love simply doesn't exist.'

'That's like saying the sky doesn't exist,' she said quietly. 'It just doesn't make sense. Did she hurt you that badly?'

He drew away from her, his eyes becoming dark.

'Yes,' he said at last, his jaw muscles clenching, 'she hurt me that badly. But it was my fault—my own stupid fault for thinking I loved her . . .'

Nicolette pulled the sheet up to cover her naked breasts, and sat up against the bulkhead, her golden skin smooth against the white of the linen.

'Tell me about it,' she said. His eyes met hers with that flat challenge she had come to know so well, but she did not flinch.

'You might as well,' she said softly. 'It's burning inside you, Alex. One day it'll burn a hole right through your heart. Please tell me.'

'Why should I waste my time and yours?' he asked, his face suddenly weary. 'It's a common enough story.'

'Because I'm nothing to you,' she said, 'because I don't matter a damn. That's why you won't mind telling me.'

Suddenly his hand was against her cheek, a caress as gentle as her father's touch, dimly remembered from far-off childhood bedtimes.

'You're not nothing to me, Nicolette,' he said in a low voice. 'You're not nothing. That's what half the trouble is.'

Her heart somersaulted inside her, and her fingers tightened on the sheet. But she knew that she must persevere, must make him tell her about Trudi—or else she would never be able to reach him again.

'Did she walk out on you?' she invited gently.

Alex smiled, a mirthless, painful smile.

'Her name was Trudi,' he said slowly. 'Trudi Reinhart. She was very beautiful. And she meant a lot to me. After we met, I—well, I suppose I went a little crazy. We decided to get married. I bought her hundreds of things—mad presents. Even a mink cape. I didn't realise what she was really like, you see. Some people tried to tell me,' he said, his eyes far away, probing into some distant hurt. 'One of my best friends tried to tell me—but I lost my temper, and hit him. I can see his face now.'

Nicolette listened in frozen silence, her heart torn. How much love must there have been to have hurt so badly, so deeply? Could Alex ever feel anything like that again? As if reading her thoughts, he smiled drily.

'It's not a feeling I ever want to have again,' he said. 'It just about destroyed my faith in human nature in the end. When I set up my factory, I had to borrow a lot of money from the bank. A hell of a lot of money. And in that first year we had a succession of disasters—a fire that destroyed some vital prototypes, a big contract fell through. Worst of all, one of our designers defected to a Belgian aerospace company, and took some of our top plans with him. Before we could do anything about that, the Belgians were in full production. It hurts, Nicolette, seeing somebody else getting rich off the design you sweated blood to perfect.'

She nodded, longing to reach out to him, but knowing she must stay silent. After a pause, Alex continued.

'Anyway, after each disaster, money got tighter and tighter. And my darling Trudi became more and more distant, more and more cool. The bank were as kind to me as they could be, but I was getting desperate. Between Trudi and the factory, my life was pretty well messed up. My dad would have helped if he could—but he was in pretty tight circumstances himself, in the middle of designing *Mistral*, and badly in need of capital.' He rubbed his cheek slowly. 'Well, the climax came when one of our contracts was foreclosed on us. We found ourselves owing nearly a million pounds in various places. I was desperate for help—even a little understanding would have done. But Trudi didn't seem to understand. She simply wanted to know where all the money had gone, where the expensive presents and good times had gone. I couldn't understand her, Nicolette. I guess that sounds crazy now—but I simply couldn't believe she was more interested in money than in me. Male vanity, I suppose,' he said with a harsh laugh. 'So I tried to explain what had happened to her. All she seemed to grasp was that there was no more money forthcoming. So she left.'

'Alex—'

'She left—with three of my latest designs in her pocket. She'd learned from that bastard who went to the Belgians, you see; and she had the brains to be able to tell a revolutionary design when she saw one. She took three designs for economy-priced light aircraft to Hal Patrides at Tempest Air Design. She presented him with them— and her body. It was an offer he couldn't turn down. So, while I was struggling along with bills for a million pounds in my pigeonholes and a broken heart, she was becoming Mrs Hal Patrides, with a mansion in Cumbria, and another in Scotland.'

There was a silence.

'And then?' Nicolette whispered. He shrugged.

'And then I pulled myself up by my boot-straps. I managed to pay my staff somehow—they were very understanding—and we got some more designs off the ground. The bank waited—bless them—and some contracts dribbled in. At the end of the last year we almost broke even. Right now, the German traffic police are considering one of my designs for a new helicopter for high-level patrolling. If they bite, that means two thousand machines over the next six months. I'm also trying to sell some executive jets to the Saudis—the sort of thing the sheiks would use to hop between meetings.'

'And Trudi?'

'We kept meeting, of course,' he said, his face an icy mask, as though he were staring into her eyes in his mind's eye. 'I never let on how badly I was hurt. That letter you were reading—that was an offer to meet me someplace. For a little extra-marital sex. I kept it,' he said drily, 'as a monument to human dignity and honesty.' He stopped a while, thinking, then went on. 'Anyway, by the time things were levelling out for Alex St Cloud and Cloud Aerospace, I was pretty well exhausted. I needed a break badly—and so my father suggested—well, to put it truth-fully,' he said, with a wry smile, 'he *ordered* me to take *Mistral* on her first sea trials. And to have a holiday at the same time. So Pete Franklin and I took her down to Kenya. Where you and your friends entered the story.'

Nicolette sighed, finding that her palms were wet.

'I'm beginning to understand why you were so furious in Mombasa,' she said. 'When I think of the way Julian and the others behaved—God, it makes my blood boil! Alex, that's an unbelievably brave story. I think you're the bravest person I've ever met.'

His eyes met hers with an ironic glint, and then he threw his head back and laughed, an amused bark that brought a smile to her own lips. 'Nicolette,' he smiled, 'what a schoolgirl you are sometimes!'

'And now I also know why you dislike women—and why you want to reduce everything to pure sex—'

'You do, do you?' he said sarcastically. There was a tiny click from the bedside table, and they both glanced at it. The travelling clock at Alex's bedside had slid against the lamp. As they watched it, it slid back again slightly, then clicked into the lamp again. Nicolette suddenly realised that *Mistral*'s motion had changed from her normal grace-ful dance-step to a heavy, plunging movement that was beginning to make Nicolette feel distinctly uncomfortable. She looked at Alex and he sighed, a look of worry appearing in his thoughtful grey eyes. 'That's the low-pressure area coming up,' he said grimly. 'I think we'd better get up on deck and batten down the hatches.' He passed her her bikini top, and turned his back. 'We'd better not have any distractions,' he said drily.

There was a cold fury in Nicolette's heart as she followed Alex up on deck. There were no words bad enough to describe Trudi Reinhart, wherever she might be. And mixed with her anger was a fierce jealousy at the thought that another woman had possessed Alex's body, had received his love. The pain of it stung her sharply, making her wince inwardly. Yet there was a glimmer of hope, too—'You're not nothing to me. That's half the trouble.' Those words were like a little flame of hope to her in the darkness up on deck.

And it was very dark. Only a yellow smear in the west showed that the sun had not yet gone down, and an eerie half-light hung over the sea. *Mistral* was still slicing through the leaden water with her knife-like prow held high; but she was beginning to pitch now, and though the waves were not yet big, there was a heavy swell that reminded her of the Atlantic, rather than the normally calm Mediterranean. They moved across the deck quickly, securing all the hatches and strapping down any loose gear. She noticed that Alex was carefully checking the little inflatable dinghy in the stern, and for the first time she realised that they might really be in for some heavy weather.

By the time they had secured *Mistral*'s decks, her sails were beginning to crack and billow in the rising wind, and Alex looked at them thoughtfully.

'Want to take them down?' she asked.

He shook his head. 'Not yet. If it gets worse, yes. Let's go and get the weather report from Crete.'

While Alex listened in, the headphones over his ears, Nicolette brewed them both a mug of cocoa in the galley. So much about Alex had become clear to her in the past half-hour that she had barely had time to absorb it. Her initial feelings about him—resentment, a schoolgirlish admiration, had given way to feelings much deeper and stronger. She could not put a name to them yet, but she could feel them stirring, deep in her heart. She carried the steaming mugs through into the wheelhouse. Alex was looking very thoughtful as he made some last notes in the log.

'Bad news?' she asked, putting the mug in his hands.

'Very. There's a gale moving this way. Fast.' He sipped from his mug, his eyes intent. 'I wonder whether we shouldn't run back to Port Said for shelter . . .'

'Are you worried?'

'I don't want to lose *Mistral*'s rigging,' he said. Then a

slight smile crossed his mouth. 'Don't think I'm casting any aspersions on your seamanship.'

'Seawomanship,' she corrected him, then grew serious. 'Couldn't we make for Alexandria, and wait there?'

'We could do.' He sighed again. 'I don't like the idea of running away, though.'

'There's nothing cowardly about being afraid of the sea,' she said gently. He met her eyes with a smile.

'As you have good reason to know, Nicolette. Yes, you're right. But it doesn't do to turn your back on the sea, either. I also hate the thought of letting Dad down.'

'Alex,' she said, unable to keep her thoughts to herself any longer, 'Trudi Reinhart—she must have been a bitch—'

'Strong language for you,' he said, raising an eyebrow.

'I feel strongly. What happened to you—' she hesitated for a moment, groping for the words, '—it doesn't mean that all women are the same. I mean—you don't have to feel—'

'I think I know what you want to tell me,' he said drily. 'You think I'm all bitter and twisted, don't you?'

'Well—'

'You're wrong, Nicolette. I'm just practical. And a lot older. Older than you are. So please—no lectures on the freshness of the human heart or whatever. Okay?' She sat, helpless and aching, and then moved her shoulders in a little shrug.

'Okay, Alex. Can I ask one more question?'

'What?'

'About Trudi. She wrote to you—that letter—' He nodded. 'Is that an invitation you've picked up? How do you feel about her now?'

'You mean, would I go running if she called me?'

'Something like that.'

He stared at her with unseeing eyes. 'Can you hate someone you once loved?'

'Not if it was real love,' she said in a small voice.

'That's a question I haven't yet found the answer to, Nicolette,' he said quietly. 'Please let's get off my private life—it's beginning to bore me. We have to think about ourselves and *Mistral* right now.' He hauled the chart from under their mugs, and drew a line with his finger across Syria. 'That's where the gale is coming from.'

'*Behind* us?' she said anxiously.

'Yes. So if we're going to run back to Egypt, we're going to have to hurry. Personally, I doubt if we'll make it. Do you want to try?'

'It's up to you, Alex,' she said, her heart yearning out to him. Their eyes met, and in the silence that followed, *Mistral* pitched with sudden violence, steadied, pitched again. Something boomed, shaking the yacht.

'It's not up to me any more,' said Alex quietly.

CHAPTER SEVEN

ALEX reached into the locker behind him and pulled out two bright orange lifejackets. He tossed her one. 'Get some jeans and a warm pullover on,' he told her, 'and then strap the lifejacket on. And don't take it off until I say so. From now on, you live, eat and sleep in it. Got that?'

Nicolette nodded and slipped down to her cabin to do as he had ordered. The lifejacket was bulky but light. Its tight presence around her chest gave added emphasis to the air of urgency that was building up steadily. When she came back to the bridge, Alex showed her the cord that hung from the front of it.

'As soon as you hit the water, you pull that. It'll inflate in about five seconds.' He pointed to the short pipe next to it. 'When the air starts leaking out, you blow into that. Understood?' She nodded again. He reached around her waist, and pulled a nylon webbing harness tight around the tops of her hips. Then he clipped a bright steel buckle into the loop on the back of it, and held up a thin, strong-looking nylon cord. 'Any time you come up out of your cabin, you hook this up.' He clipped the other end of the cord on to a metal bolt that was sunk into the deck. 'Come on—let's take some of that canvas down.'

The rising wind was making the sails hard to handle, and the steel guys burned Nicolette's hands as they doused the spinnaker. Alex dragged the big sail down the companionway.

The sea was rolling now. It was almost pitch black, and in the darkness, the wind was beginning to howl, hurling the salt spray across *Mistral*'s decks. Nicolette was grateful for the nylon lifeline that secured her to the motherly presence of the yacht. She had been in gales before, in the Channel, and she had a fair idea of what to expect. If all went well, *Mistral* should weather the storm without difficulty. And the big wind was blowing them steadily towards Gibraltar—the way home. In the wheelhouse, she lit the hurricane lamp, and Alex came up from below into the soft yellow light.

'Good girl! I'm going to get the engines started now. There's not much we can do except sit tight.'

The comforting throb of the engines began under her feet, a sound just beneath the threshold of the wind's howl. *Mistral* was pitching and rolling at the same time now, an eerie sensation which was uncomfortable, but not yet actually alarming. Alex flipped a switch on the complicated electronics board beside the wheel.

'Radar deflector,' he told her briefly. 'Most of the electrics on the ship come from my factory. Did you notice that mesh plate on the mast? That ought to reflect anyone else's radar, making a blip on their screen, and telling them we're here. I'm going to use our radar too—for what it's worth.'

She came to stand beside him. The radar screen was a circular glass panel; a radiating line revolved constantly in it, like the accelerated hand of a clock, and anything larger than a dinghy would show up as a blob of light. 'With the bad weather, freak waves may show up as blips from time to time,' he warned her, 'and if there's any electrical disturbance, that'll show up as ghosting.' He tapped the screen. 'It's worth keeping an eye on, though. The field is good—I designed the system myself—and it ought to give us warning of anything in our area up to fifty miles away.' Nicolette nodded her understanding, and boxed the compass. Then she nestled on the settee, wrapping a blanket around herself, as Alex took the wheel. She watched him, a tall, dark figure in the soft light, his legs planted firmly on the deck, strong hands resting lightly on the wheel. How far they had come since that afternoon in Serengeti when he had jumped out of the white Range Rover, and she had run into his arms, covered in the red mud of Kenya! This journey on *Mistral* had been like a voyage into someone else's life. And also like a voyage into her own heart. How many of her expectations and dreams had been altered since that day! Suddenly she laughed softly.

'What's so funny?' asked Alex without turning his head.

'I was just thinking of your remark a few days ago—"I'm afraid the Red Sea is rather short on roses." It seems kind of funny now.'

She knew he was smiling.

The wind had risen steadily, and she awoke from a light doze to find that *Mistral* was tossing like a leaf in a gale. And she was feeling somewhat uneasy in the middle. Alex was still at the wheel, and she rose to step beside him.

'Want some cocoa?'

'That sounds good,' he said, twisting his neck tiredly. She glanced at him, worried. It was nearly nine, and he had been at the wheel for a long time. She walked through to the galley, losing her balance several times as the yacht plunged downwards and then up again. And in the galley, things were behaving very oddly. Three small saucepans scuttled across a shelf like mad things, and leaped into the sink with a clatter. Various unsecured objects in the freezer had begun to jostle one another with inanimate resentment, and the milk from the cocoa-pan suddenly leaped gracefully into the air to cascade in a white splash all over the stove. Nicolette wiped up the mess, shifting her stance like a boxer, and tried again. With more attention this time, she succeeded in making two large cups of the comforting brew, and she carried them gingerly through to the bridge, managing to spill not more than half the contents on the way.

The movement of the boat was beginning to seriously disagree with her, and she sipped her cocoa with a rising gorge. Surely something as harmless as cocoa wasn't going to make her sick? Perhaps the milk was sour? She sniffed at it. Yes, it had a distinctly odd smell, like—like—

She rose hastily, feeling a general rising sensation inside her, and stepped towards the door. Alex reached out and tugged her back.

'In the sink,' he said briefly, and she tottered back to the galley, feeling horribly sick. She leaned on the sink, in the grip of a deadly nausea. The pitching of the ship was horrible, a movement that was making the backs of her eyeballs ache. A little casserole dish sprang with ridiculous grace off the edge of a shelf, and shattered against the bulkhead.

At all costs, she must fight her seasickness—she couldn't leave Alex to battle it out alone. She staggered around in the galley, trying to secure what had straps or clips on it, thrusting whatever was loose into cupboards. Then she was sick.

Feeling marginally better, she washed her face clumsily at the taps and made her way back to the bridge. In the gentle yellow light of the hurricane lamp, she and Alex were in a world apart from the rest of the universe. The Perspex windows were pitch-black, and they might have been tumbling through empty space together but for the thunder of the storm and the waves that crashed on to the windows from time to time.

'Are we going to be all right?' she asked, and saw the glint in Alex's grin.

'This is nothing,' he assured her. '*Mistral* was designed for weather like this.' But he looked tired now, the level eyes becoming misty.

'Alex, let me take the wheel for a bit,' she pleaded. He hesitated, then shook his head.

'I'll be fine,' he told her. 'I could do this all night.'

'And all to-morrow? And all the next day?' He did not reply. 'Let me steer her, Alex. It was always one of the things I was good at.' He looked at her quickly, grey eyes probing hers in the half-light. The he stepped back to let her take the wheel. She gasped as the thick wooden spokes stirred under her fingers. The wheel was possessed of a ferocious life of its own now.

'That's my boat you've got there,' said Alex quietly. 'Don't do anything silly.'

She shook her head, bracing her arms. The smooth columns in her hands tugged and strained with incredible force, threatening to pull her over to one side, then suddenly changing direction, and making her stagger.

'The currents are fierce,' he told her, 'besides everything else. This is our course,' he said, tapping the pointer on the compass. 'Just keep her steady. Think you can do it?'

She nodded again, stifling a gasp as the wheel thrust her sideways. Alex stepped behind her, pressing her elbows down. 'You don't have to hold it rigid,' he said. 'Give her a bit of play. Get your legs apart more.'

Nicolette obeyed, straddling her legs in the way she had seen Alex do, her sea-boots planted firmly apart, her arms more relaxed. 'How's that?' he asked after a few seconds.

'Better,' she nodded.

'Good. I'm going to the galley to make some coffee. Just yell if you need help.'

'Okay.'

She stared out of the black window ahead. If he knew how very frightened she was, he might not have left her with the wheel at all! She fought her fear down angrily, and concentrated on the heavy mahogany wheel. The sense of responsibility was alarming at first, but she quickly lost herself in the complexities of controlling the wheel. The thick spokes in her palms were like living parts of some struggling creature that strained and thrust against her will. She realised that she was at the very heart of *Mistral*, trying to impose her wishes on the beautiful yacht's proud spirit. Her terror changed slowly to an abiding excitement. There was a fine art to steering, to anticipating the powerful surges and thrusts of the boat's movements, and using her own strength and resilience to respond to them. She checked the compass carefully, swinging the wheel with firm, light movements to pull *Mistral*'s head round.

But it was hard work; soon she began to feel as if every muscle in her body was being strained and twisted. The slender muscles that ran down her sides began to ache, and her wrists were feeling the strain.

'To the manner born,' Alex murmured drily behind her. He reached past her and engaged the auto-pilot. 'We can let George take over for a few minutes while you drink your coffee. But we can't leave the auto on for too long in this weather—it might strain the gear.'

Her arms were aching as they sat on the settee, bracing their backs against the bulkhead, and the hand that held her coffee-mug was trembling. Alex smiled ironically— but also with something like respect. 'You looked as though you were rather enjoying that,' he said.

'I was,' she confessed, grinning. 'It's a big thrill, steer-ing *Mistral*!'

'Let's hope it's as big as thrill when the storm *really* breaks,' he said calmly, draining his mug. She stared at him, aghast.

'You mean it's going to get *worse*?'

'Worse? Certainly. It's going to get considerably worse than this.' He smiled at her. 'This is merely the prelude to the main movement.'

Nicolette awoke with the feeling that something was horribly wrong. She had gone down to her cabin to sleep at about midnight, leaving Alex with the wheel. How long had she slept? She checked her watch. Nearly six a.m.! He had been at the wheel all night! She staggered to her feet, a renewed bout of sickness seizing her, and making her groan. And then, suddenly, there was that horrible feel-ing again, a long, sickening drop, as though Mistral had fallen off the edge of the world. Her heart thudding. Nicolette ran up the companionway, the lurching of the yacht thumping her painfully against the bulkhead as she went.

The darkness of the night had been replaced with an eerie grey light. As she tripped into the wheelhouse, she saw Alex hauling at the wheel, the bronzed muscles on his arms standing out with the strain. She ran over to him. The floor of the bridge was awash with sea-water, and she cannoned into him, her sea-boots slipping, and her arms flung themselves around his hard waist. She could feel the flat muscles of his stomach tensing under her hands. And then she stared out of the window in terror, gasping at the impossible sight that met her eyes—a vertical sheet of green seawater patterned with racing white foam. Her first absurd, terrified thought was that they had sunk; and then the deck heaved upwards against her, and the gigantic wave began to level out as they reached the peak of it. She clung to Alex as the spray crashed over *Mistral's* decks.

She had time to glimpse a hideous world of driving rain and mist, peopled with massive green mountains, before she became rigid with frozen disbelief again. They were at the top of an unbelievably long valley of seawater, a livid green slope that yawned open like some vision of Hell in a mediaeval painting. And now they were racing down it with ghastly speed, heading for the maelstrom at the bottom. As they hurtled into the abyss, Nicolette buried her mouth against Alex's hard shoulder, watching with terrified eyes as the mountain of water, impossibly vast, gathered above them. She squeezed her eyes shut, grateful in some tiny corner of her soul that she was at least with Alex, that they were going to be buried under that terrible mass of water together—

Again the deck heaved up under their feet, and *Mistral* was shooting up the side of the wave like a paper boat in a millrace.

'Where are we?' she gasped, holding him with desperate arms.

'Somewhere off Greece,' he answered, his voice thick with exhaustion. 'It's hard to tell—the compass isn't working properly.'

She swung round to stare into his face, noting the lines of strain around eyes and mouth. His mouth flickered into a smile. 'Are you scared?'

'Terrified,' she answered, trying to respond to his smile. 'Are we going to die?'

'Not this year,' he answered with dry amusement, his eyes flicking to the sea ahead. 'God, I'm tired—and starving—'

'I'll make you something to eat,' she said, deciding that it was best not even to look out of the window. 'Bacon and eggs?'

'You're an angel,' he nodded. 'And be careful with the cooker—and with hot oil.' Nicolette waited until *Mistral* had reached the top of one of the huge waves, and then ran back to the galley.

Making breakfast was an almost impossible task. The best thing, she discovered after various painful mishaps, was to hold the saucepan over the gas-ring, tilting it hastily to compensate for *Mistral*'s plungings. That way, she assembled a greasy mess of bacon and eggs, hacked off some chunks of bread, and sandwiched the meal between two plates. Then waiting for the right moment, she dashed back to the bridge.

'I'll take the wheel,' she called, but Alex shook his head.

'It's too rough—you won't be able to hold it. We'll try George.' He engaged the auto-pilot, and stood back experimentally. *Mistral* shuddered her way to the top of the next wave more or less uneventfully, and Alex slumped back into the little pilot's chair with a sigh of relief. She clung to his arm for stability in the rollercoaster motion of the cabin, and he ate slowly, his face tired and set.

'Aren't you having any?' he enquired. Nicolette shook her head, feeling queasy at the thought.

'I'd better keep my stomach empty till I feel a bit better.' He smiled, examining the greasy egg on his plate.

'I don't blame you.'

'Is this normal?' she asked, pointing to the huge seas outside.

'Not exactly,' he replied thoughtfully. 'I've never known anything like this in the Mediterranean before. These are freak conditions. This storm will be causing havoc all over Europe.' In the weird grey light, she saw that his face was worried.

'Have a little rest,' she pleaded. 'I'll keep an eye on the wheel.'

Alex rubbed the back of his neck, plainly exhausted. 'All right,' he said at last. 'Don't try and take the wheel —just wake me if anything starts going wrong— okay?'

She nodded, took his plate, and helped him to his feet. The movement of the sea threw them across the wheel-house together, and she collapsed back against the settee, drawing herself into a corner against the far bulkhead. She braced herself against the padded back-rest, and opened her arms to Alex. After a moment's hesitation, he came to her and lay in her arms, his head cradled on her breast.

Nicolette held him close, lost in the weight of his body against her, his man-smell in her nostrils. After a while she could feel the big body relax, and he began to breathe deeply and evenly. She stared over his head at the vast seas outside the little panel that separated them from the storm, trying to protect him from the rolling of the yacht. He slept.

Nicolette's thoughts were in a turmoil. This terrible gale, she knew, might claim both their lives at any minute. Yet she was still confused, still uncertain about this big, strong man lying so peacefully in her arms. She was here now because she had chosen to come with him, had forced herself into his life. Why? Now, in this maelstrom, somewhere off Greece, in the midst of a huge gale, her own actions had begun to puzzle her. So many questions were forming in her mind. Why had she cut off her hair? Why had she been so desperate to get away from *Elsie*? And when Mark had confessed to her about Geraldine, how had she really felt? Wounded? Relieved? Now was a fine time to start soul-searching, in these fraught moments that might be her last! She lay puzzling her way through the maze of her thoughts for almost an hour, as Alex slept on, and *Mistral* plunged onward through chasms and cliffs of seawater.

The weather was, if anything, getting worse. From time to time, hail was rattling across *Mistral*'s decks like gunfire, and her movement was changing from the horrible but relatively smooth up-and-down motion to a shuddering, heavy surge and fall, that reminded her of some big animal stuck in sinking sand. It was this which eventually woke Alex. He stirred out of her arms, shaking his head.

'How are you feeling?' she asked, finding that she was now having to shout above the noise of the gale.

'Better,' he called back. Then he leaned forward and kissed her on the mouth, a quick, rough caress, before he stepped across to take the wheel and disengage the auto-pilot. With his kiss still tingling on her mouth, Nicolette stumbled back to the galley to make some more coffee. By the time she was bringing the steaming brew back, *Mistral* was staggering heavily through the raging sea. The huge waves were no longer smooth and glistening, but had become broken and rough. And when the grey yacht reached the tops of the waves, she no longer slipped easily over the edge, but had begun to plough under, her proud nose sinking into the white water, so that she staggered drunkenly, and cascades poured over her decks. The yacht was trembling violently, as though her very wooden soul were being tormented, and at each new assault, she had begun to creak and groan frighteningly. Alex was wrestling with the wheel, and his face was beginning to shine with sweat. She could see the muscles standing out in thick cords across his arms and shoulders. *Mistral* plunged heavily into the foaming water, her prow sub-merging almost completely, sending Nicolette and her coffee flying across the wheelhouse. As the sea cascaded across the yacht's white decks, Nicolette could see that the brass guard-rail on the prow had been torn away. Alex swore briefly; and then, with another horrible shudder, the big yacht plunged back into a second wave coming hard on the heels of the first. There was a long tearing sound that set Nicolette's teeth on edge, the yacht seemed to plunge in agony, and then the wheel was whirling uselessly in Alex's hands, and *Mistral* was spinning helplessly sideways up the white face of the next cliff.

'What's happened?' she screamed.

He turned to her, his face white with tiredness and frustration.

'The steering gear's gone,' he said tersely. 'We've lost our rudder.' They stared at one another. Nicolette's heart began to beat heavily against her ribs.

'You mean—we can't steer *Mistral* any more? What will happen to us, Alex?'

'We're going to have to wait and see,' he said briefly. In the silence that followed, the yacht slewed dizzily across the top of a wave, and careened wildly down the long slope to the abyss below. Nicolette found herself in Alex's arms, crushed against his chest. His voice was a deep rumble in her ear.

'Nicolette, I'm so sorry. You shouldn't be here—'

'I chose to be here,' she said, raising her head to look at him through swimming eyes. 'I'd rather go down with you than live without you, Alex.'

'We're not going down yet,' he said, his grey eyes holding hers with all the power in his spirit. 'There's still—'

He broke off. A shrill electronic alarm signal had begun to sound through the wheelhouse. They ran to the radar screen, in time to see the signal pass over a large green blip, leaving a trail of viridian fire behind it. As they watched, the signal came round again, and once again the green ember glowed in the dark panel.

'A ship,' she said.

'Yes. A big ship,' he confirmed, staring at the panel with set lips.

'Is it coming our way?' she demanded.

'Wait.' He switched off the alarm, and then punched buttons on the panel. *Mistral* spun crazily up the slope of a wave, making them stagger and clutch at one another.

'Yes,' said Alex quietly. 'It's coming our way.'

'Will they see us?'

'Maybe. These waves are higher than *Mistral*'s mast, Nicolette—we're just going to show up as an intermittent flash on their screens—if we show up at all, that is.' He stooped, and clipped their lifelines to the bolt in the deck. 'I'm going to send up a flare. They might just see that.' She watched the green spark on the radar screen as he broke out the flare-pistol from the locker next to the wheel. The ship was drawing steadily closer. It would be steaming doggedly into the teeth of the gale, she guessed, some iron-hulled cargo ship trying to run right through the bad weather.

'Hold on, Nicolette!' He wrenched the wheelhouse door open, and suddenly the howling gale was inside, a fury of wind and lashing rain that blotted out sight and hearing. The sea crashed around her ankles as she clung to the wheelhousing. Alex had looped one arm around the door post; he fired the flare pistol into the gale, and within a few seconds a dim red light glowed in the filthy sky overhead, flickered, and drifted out into the darkness beyond. He fired three more times, with the same result, and then half-fell back into the wheelhouse, hauling the door shut behind him.

'Will they see them?' she asked.

He shook water off himself, and stared through the window.

'I doubt it,' he admitted. 'The wind's so strong, it's just carrying the flares away. Even if they do see something, they won't be able to tell where we are.' She looked at him with huge brown eyes, and he smiled gently, then came over to take her in his arms. 'You've been so brave,' he said tenderly, ruffling her golden curls and smiling into her eyes, 'no one could have done better than you. I'm afraid there's nothing we can do, my dear. We're just going to have to pray that it misses us. Okay?'

'Okay,' she said, holding him close, and wishing that the lifejackets weren't coming between their bodies. She rested her head in the crook of his arm as he braced his legs against the yacht's plummeting. Holding each other tight, they watched the green blip on the radar screen, drawing inexorably nearer and nearer. They could only see a few yards beyond *Mistral*'s damaged prow now. The air had turned into a whirling inferno of rain and hail. And the big grey yacht, rudderless, wallowed in the troughs and rolled up the peaks, waiting with them.

Nicolette searched her mind for a few prayers, trying to control the terror in her heart. And slowly, a new feeling began to spread through her—a profound peace that she could not at first recognise. Her arms were tight around Alex's supple waist, his own arms strong and protective around her. She watched the green ember in the screen, glowing like some alien pulse, telling them of the danger that was steaming towards them in the heart of the storm, and found that her fear was slipping away from her like a bad dream. She knew now that her feelings about Alex were clear. She loved him. It was so very simple, so blindingly obvious, that she was almost puzzled at her own inability to see it. She watched the green blip absently, wondering when she had first begun to fall in love with him. Could it have begun that afternoon in Serengeti? No, that was silly. Yet it *had* begun there—the long journey that had brought her to this realisation, to this time and place—had begun in the wilderness of Serengeti. In another storm.

She looked up into his face, awestruck at the depth of her own emotion. His eyes were fixed on the lashing rain outside, wonderful, magnificent eyes that could command like an emperor, caress like sunshine. She reached up and touched his mouth, the passionate, proud lips that had shown her so much about herself on this short journey. Alex looked down at her, his eyes fathomless. She opened her mouth, wanting to tell him what she had just learned, but he kissed her lips shut, holding her close.

'We're going to be all right,' he said.

A long blast rose above the sound of the storm, the savage warning cry of some big ship. Simultaneously, they stared out into the storm, and then at the radar screen. The emerald was glowing almost at the core of the panel now, so brightly that it was trailing a ring of sinister fire round the centre of the sweep. Again, the foghorn boomed out of the whirling gale, closer now. Alex's arms were like steel around her, almost crushing the air out of her lungs. They stood rigid, clinging together, their eyes fixed on the surging sea ahead.

And then the chaos outside darkened swiftly. Something vast loomed out of the driving hail, a gigantic steel blade with white foam in its teeth. The bow-wave rocked *Mistral* back on her heels, and the massive black-and-red prow surged towards them, ramming on through the wild sea. They were close enough to see the rivets that joined her plates, the streaks of rust on her hull, the long line of flaking white numerals that ran down into the water.

Unable to look, Nicolette buried her face in Alex's chest. The world tilted, shuddered, fell.

She came to her senses in a panic, her lungs full of salt water that burned like fire. It was pitch-black, and she was aware of various pains. *Where was he?* She realised that she was sprawling across the port bulkheads, being rolled painfully across the Perspex windows with half a ton of seawater and a collection of smashed debris. *Mistral* was on her side.

Then the yacht slowly began to heel over again, sending Nicolette tumbling down across the settee, whose leather cushions had now vanished in the general chaos in the wheelhouse. She crashed into the deck with a bone-jarring thud, spewing salt water and retching. The wheelhouse door was open, and a sudden torrent hurtled in, slamming her backwards, and pouring down the companionway into the heart of the yacht. Then she saw Alex, hauling himself back into the wheelhouse by his lifeline. She scrambled over to him, sobbing, and helped him to slam the wheelhouse door shut against the invading storm. Then she threw her aching arms around his neck, and cried.

'Hush,' he said roughly, holding her tenderly, close, 'we're going to be all right.'

CHAPTER EIGHT

MISTRAL limped on through the storm for days, the big winds blowing her inexorably towards Spain. The cargo ship, Nicolette discovered, had not hit them. Not quite. Its massive bow-wave had sent the grey yacht sprawling into the troughs until the weight of *Mistral*'s own huge keel had pulled her upright again.

The storm began to peter out, and Alex hoisted sail as the winds died down, and steered her that way until he could find or make replacement parts for the broken gear from *Mistral*'s collection of spares. But there was other damage which could not be repaired. The radio mast had been carried off by the hungry sea when the yacht had capsized, and they could no longer receive messages. Their transmissions were limited to Morse signals on the emergency handset. They listened to the local weather reports on Nicolette's transistor radio.

Like the yacht, she and Alex both carried the marks of the gale—bruises and cuts, mysterious sprains and aches that had come from being battered against various parts of *Mistral*'s structure. But the new knowledge that Nicolette carried was a sweet, joyful ache that dominated everything else. She felt as though she had come alive for the first time in her adult life—had come to full woman-hood. She was excited, delighted, endlessly in love with Alex. She could not take her eyes off him for long hours, coming to find him with joyous eyes and a smile that was transforming her face into loveliness. Alex watched her in turn with fathomless eyes, as though wondering what had changed her so much over the passage of the storm. They worked together as a flawless team now, their thoughts at one with another to such an extent that sometimes they barely needed to speak in order to communicate their wishes. A timid sun had emerged from the wet haze by the time *Mistral* was ploughing through the Straits of Gibraltar, the gateway to the Atlantic, and as they rounded Cadiz, Nicolette was lying on the deck, blissfully soaking up the heat in her bikini. Her heart was bursting with the excitement of her love for Alex; she longed to tell him, to be in his arms, to let him take her now, as he had wanted to that night in the Red Sea.

Yet her instincts kept her from saying anything to him, or even from showing him by her expression how deeply she felt. She sensed that he was wary of her, needed to think about her, and her fine intuition kept her from trying to force him into any acknowledgment of how she felt. Alex was a free spirit—as free as the beautiful grey yacht that was carrying her home so swiftly now; she must never try to chain him, try to hold him down. He would simply shake her off as *Mistral* shook off the impeding waves, and be gone. But if he came to her—no, she corrected herself with an inner smile, *when* he came to her—it would be for ever. The passion in Alex, the need to love and be loved, was vast, a surging power like the power of the sea.

She lay basking in the sun, feeling its golden fingers easing the aches out of her body. They had both eaten little over the days of the gale, and she had made up for it by feeding them both as magnificently as she could now that the glorious sun was back. Her body was like a new machine, refined, honed down to its essentials, as beautiful and elegant as any other of Nature's creations. When they were back in England, she promised herself, she was going to spend some money on new clothes for herself. She was longing for the feel of cool material against her skin instead of the bikini and T-shirt which were her usual attire, and which had begun to fade through so much washing. She glanced at the heavy silver hoop around her golden wrist. Alex's slave—yes, he would make her his slave, she knew that, with that magnificent body, with the passion he would arouse in her . . . She shook the thought away, feeling hot, and thought about clothes. As for her hair—well, that was simply going to have to grow.

The sky was blue above them, not the deep cobalt of an African sky, but the soft, warm blue of a European sky, flecked with one or two wisps of white cloud. The warmth was so delicious. Nicolette raised herself on one elbow. Alex was at the taffrail, wearing only a black bathing costume, bolting a new length of the brass rail back into place. On an impulse, she stood up and came over to him. The brown and green coast of Spain was to their right, the air carrying the faint hot smell of summer from the land out to sea. She stood next to him, the light breeze ruffling her golden hair, watching him work with quiet brown eyes. There was a long violet smudge down Alex's right shoulder, a reminder of where *Mistral*'s deck had crashed into the hard muscles during those horrible minutes after the near-collision. It gave her a pang to think of his pain, and she reached out a golden hand and ran her forefinger lightly across the bruise in the mahogany flesh.

Alex stiffened, the big muscles tensing quickly under the velvety skin, and then he turned to face her, a deep amethyst light in his eyes. Her stomach plunged, and she smiled up at him uncertainly.

'Hullo,' she said in a small voice, her heart aching for him. His smile was slow, thrilling; but there was a tension in him that she could not understand—as though she were his enemy—a dangerous enemy who had to be watched and guarded against. It would take a great deal, she knew, to rid him of his deep-rooted distrust of women. And then the wind was heavy with the smell of roses—the unbelievable, heady, sweet smell of big summer roses in full bloom. She blinked in amazement, and raised her nose to sniff the sweet air luxuriously. Alex laughed.

'It sometimes happens,' he said gently. 'There are huge fields of roses in the South of Spain—grown for the perfume trade. Now and then, when the wind is right, the smell of them carries out to sea. Someone once told me he could smell them in the middle of the Atlantic.'

'Imagine what it must be like in the middle of those fields,' she smiled, looking into the splendour of his eyes. Her smile faded slowly. Alex's eyes were turning her heart over, making her weak at the knees. Suddenly she couldn't look into them any more, and she dropped her head, reaching out an uncertain hand to rest against the crisp dark curls on his broad chest.

'Alex—' she said, her throat dry. 'I—' His arms slid round her waist slowly, almost unwillingly, and he drew her gently to him, so that their near-naked bodies were touching, and she could feel the warmth of his skin, smell the salty, musky tang of his skin. She looked up, losing herself in the grey depths of his eyes. He stooped to kiss her—a firm, hard kiss on the lips that was a rejection as well as a caress.

'Go and sunbathe, little virgin,' he said firmly.

'But, Alex—'

'I have work to do,' he said with a gentle smile.

She met his eyes boldly, her heart beating. 'Then why don't you let me go?' she asked with a daring smile. There was a rueful glint in his face.

'What do you want, Nicolette?' he asked gently.

She took a deep breath. 'A kiss,' she said simply.

'Go on, then.' The flat challenge was back in his eyes. She hesitated, then reached around his strong neck, stood on tiptoe, and kissed him shyly on the mouth. He shook with laughter, and she coloured, angry and embarrassed.

'My poor schoolgirl,' he said mockingly, 'you kiss like a child saying goodnight to a strange uncle!'

'Teach me, then,' she retorted.

He shook his head calmly. 'I'm too old for you, Nicolette. Too old and hard and cynical.'

Abruptly, she reached up again, pulling his head towards her, and pressed her mouth against his, fiercely determined to make him respond to her. His arms tightened around her, and then his mouth took hers, with a passion that shook her. She could feel his desire surging against her, and she shuddered in his arms, digging her nails into his shoulders, willing him to take her completely, utterly. She gasped when he thrust her back, his eyes dark with anger.

'For God's sake,' he snapped, his voice shaky, 'what are you trying to do to me, Nicolette?'

She stood in front of him, aching, puzzled. 'Alex, I want—'

'You don't know what you want,' he told her angrily, his voice still uneven. 'Don't play with me, Nicolette. Go and sunbathe.' He turned his back on her, and locked the heavy rail into place with one powerful movement. It was no consolation to her, as she turned slowly away, to know that those strong brown hands were trembling slightly.

The last few days of their journey were full of sunshine. Alex was kept busy with minor repairs all over *Mistral*, and Nicolette helped him where she could. And then one morning, the long white line of England was in sight before them. Alex had used the hand-transmitter to send a message to his father, telling him that they would be bringing *Mistral* in to the St Cloud boatyard at Plymouth, and with a suddenness that depressed Nicolette, the long journey on the grey yacht was drawing to a close. She leaned on the winch at the prow as *Mistral* sailed triumphantly into Plymouth Harbour round Rame Head, her feelings a confused mixture of happiness and misery. The idea of parting from Alex tore at her heart. She *must* see him again! The wheeling, mewing gulls that ushered them in seemed to be calling goodbye so piercingly that her eyes were blurred with tears. In the bustle and confusion of docking, and giving *Mistral* back to Paul St Cloud, would she have a chance of telling Alex that she wanted to keep on seeing him? She stared dimly at the approaching pier, trying not to cry, her straw hat fluttering in her hand. Then she blinked.

There seemed to be a small crowd at the boatyard. And as *Mistral* sailed majestically into the haven, a ragged cheer went up from the few hundred people on the pier.

'Don't just stand there,' called Alex, 'come and give me a hand with these sails!'

'Who are all those people?' she asked breathlessly as they folded the big sails into neat bundles.

He glanced up, then frowned.

'I've no idea.' He squinted at two big white lorries parked on the quayside, and read, 'BBC Outside Broadcast Team'. They looked at one another in puzzlement. As *Mistral* slipped alongside the stone pier, Alex threw the mooring-rope ashore, and eager hands secured the grey yacht fore and aft. The beautiful, gull-like yacht was still at last, bobbing quietly in the murky waters, as though the journey of nearly four thousand miles and twelve days had never been. A few Union Jacks were waving in the crowd of people gaping at them as they walked ashore.

'Welcome home to Britain, Mr St Cloud,' called a reporter, stepping in front of a television camera. 'How does it feel to be back?'

Alex stared around with cold eyes. 'What's all this?' he asked sharply. Nicolette came to join him in bewilderment, the solid ground feeling weirdly unsteady beneath her feet after all those days at sea.

'Miss Mercury,' said the reporter, thrusting the microphone under her nose, 'were you frightened during the storm?'

'I—how do you know about the storm?' she asked, glancing in astonishment at the whirring cameras and flashing bulbs. Someone else was talking now, telling them they were national heroes, that the nation had been following their progress with keen interest—

Abruptly, they were swamped with people, asking, demanding, recording, filming. Nicolette felt a hard little hand clutch her elbow, and an attractive, beautifully-dressed woman in her forties was pulling her aside.

'Anita Jensen, *Sunday Magazine*,' she said in a businesslike voice. 'Don't speak to anyone, Nicky—not until you hear our terms.'

'Your terms for what?' she gasped.

'Contract. Your story, of course,' said Anita Jensen, elbowing a sister reporter neatly out of the way. 'Five instalments at two thousand apiece. How's that? "How I Saved My Lover's Life in the Storm", that sort of thing. You won't have to write a word of it,' she added confidentially. 'Got a camera? Take any pictures? Never mind, we'll mug some up in no time—'

Nicolette pulled her arm furiously out of the reporter's hand, and tried to fight her way through the crowd back to Alex. Another microphone appeared under her nose.

'Did you have any idea of the interest with which British audiences were following your progress, Miss Mercury?'

'None at all,' she gasped, trying to get away. She could see Alex's father trying to reach him through the ring of reporters and curious sightseers. A newspaper was thrust into her hands, and she stared at it in confusion. LOVERS LOST? screamed the headline. Most of the article consisted of two blurred pictures, one of her in a bikini (where on earth had that come from?) and another of Alex getting out of a helicopter. The article began,

'Runaway lovers Alex St Cloud and Nicolette Mercury were feared lost last night after the heavy gale that has been battering Europe crossed their last reported position . . .'

She glanced at the date in horror—a week ago. She dropped the paper, only to catch sight of a banner poster

for this morning's *Echo*: RUNAWAY LOVERS RE-
TURN SAFELY.

'Please say something for our viewers,' demanded a
middle-aged woman with a vast, toothy smile, waving not
one but two microphones in front of her.

'What's your birth sign, Nicky?' called a young reporter
from behind her.

'I don't want to say anything!' she answered in confusion, looking around for Alex, who was trying to free
himself from the attentions of the television crew.

And then a tall, exquisitely beautiful woman with long
chestnut hair came through the crowd, pulling off dark
glasses to reveal deep blue eyes.

'Alex!' she called in a thrilling voice.

Alex spun round, a strange expression crossing his face.
His hands dropped to his sides.

'Hullo, Trudi,' he said quietly.

'*Alex!*' she repeated, her contralto voice breaking with
emotion. She ran to him, dropping the glasses to break on
the stones, and threw her arms round his neck, wildly
pressing her scarlet lips to his.

Nicolette watched in frozen, numbed horror as Alex's
arms came up slowly to encircle the woman's elegant
waist as the kiss grew more passionate, and her red-nailed
fingers disappeared into his dark hair.

'Alex—' Nicolette gasped. He did not hear her. A
reporter shouted, 'Turn this way, Miss Reinhart,' and
cameras began to focus hastily. A flashbulb exploded in
Nicolette's face. Anita Jensen was at her side again,
persistent little claw tugging at Nicolette's wrist..

'The treacherous bastard!' she hissed with bright eyes.
'Aren't men all the same? That's Trudi Patrides, Nicky—

know her? Never mind, you will. Listen, we'll make it two thousand five hundred for the instalments. And an extra article—"My Bitter Homecoming"—to wind up the series. What do you say? That'll be damn near thirteen thousand all told, not to mention the picture rights—'

Nicolette wasn't listening. Her brown eyes were fixed with disbelief on the glamorous couple who were kissing so passionately in front of a suddenly galvanised audience of cameras and reporters. Kissing with the expert sexual awareness of long-established partners. Kissing with the hunger of long separation. Kissing away her hopes, her dreams, her life.

When the telephone had started ringing at six-thirty in the morning, memory had returned scaldingly to Nicolette. She scarcely remembered the long train journey back to London yesterday, or what she had done last night. All she remembered was the ache that had begun yesterday morning, and that was hurting even more to-day.

She went out once, to buy some groceries, disguised in dark glasses and scarf to avoid questions, and had returned with a handful of the daily papers, in an effort to piece together what the papers had been saying since she and Alex had left Mombasa together. It was the huge gale, of course, which had brought them to public attention. The terrible weather had, as Alex had predicted, been smashing towns all over Europe; and the idea of two people alone in a yacht, facing the devastation together, had somehow seized the public imagination. The newspapers had spiced the story with as much sex as they could rake up. Alex was 'devastatingly handsome aero-designer' and she was 'gorgeous blonde art restorer'. The papers had been divided in their reactions to *Mistral*'s homecoming. Some had stuck loyally to the RUNAWAY LOVERS HOME AT LAST story. Others had gone for PIPPED AT THE POST—ALEX'S EX STEPS IN, and carried big photographs of The Kiss. One had a shot of her own horrified face as she stared at Trudi Reinhart (or Patrides, no one was sure which) kissing Alex.

In the absence of any solid story, most of the papers had restored to pictures. Oddly enough, the Rubens figured in many of them, no doubt because it showed two voluptuous nudes, and invited suitably arch commentary about 'Playboy Alex St Cloud' and his two women.

The Times had put them on the front page—but simply as BRITONS BACK SAFELY. Bless its stiff upper lip! She had not dared switch on her little portable television set.

And at lunchtime, there was a knock on the door. Unguardedly, she went to open it.

'Ralph Johnson,' said the immaculately-suited man, pressing his card into her hand, '*Fungirls* magazine. We'd like to do a nude series with you, Miss Mercury—'

She slammed the door, resolving not to open it again.

But her little house fronted on to Hampstead Heath, and in the afternoon she ventured through her garden on to the Heath, and wandered round for an hour, gazing unseeingly at dogs and children. She would have to get back to work, she supposed. There had been a pile of new commissions waiting on her doormat, though she hadn't had the heart to read through them all yet. Work was her panacea for all ills. If only her father were still alive to comfort her, advise her. She thought of those red-nailed hands burying themselves so intimately into Alex's hair.

Alex's thick, dark hair, still stiff with salt and over-long after twelve days at sea in a racing yacht. The pain intensified. She had not bargained for Trudi. Nor for Trudi's stunning beauty. There was something glamorous about her, a sexy quality which she guessed men would find very hard to resist. And Alex—so strong and hard—would he be one of the men who succumbed?

Would I go running to her if she called me? That's a question I haven't yet found the answer to, Nicolette.

She was going to have to wait. Like she had waited for news of her father during that terrible week. And inside her, the knowledge that he was gone, would never come back to her, would never be found.

Across the Heath she spotted Arnold, an old friend. Arnold was a paper-boy, a mentally handicapped man in his late sixties, whose pale blue eyes looked on the world with ineffable gentleness, and whose loose, foolish mouth always wore a slight smile. Arnold was a favourite of Nicolette's, one of the people whose conversation never bored her. She walked over to him, to be greeted with a wide grin and a wave of joy.

'Hullo, Arnold,' she smiled, shaking the soft hand.

'I seen about you in the papers, miss,' he said with quiet excitement. 'You and Mister Angelcloud.'

'That's right, Arnold,' she said wryly. 'Me and Mister Angelcloud.'

'You're in it again tonight,' he said eagerly, rolling a newspaper up and offering it to her. 'Fourteen pence,' he added in a businesslike tone.

She smiled and gave him a pound.

'Keep the change, Arnie—for being the only person in Britain to smile at me when I came home.'

Arnold beamed with delight, and tapped the paper.

'Read about Mister Angelcloud,' he urged her, nodding happily. 'You'll be pleased!'

Nicolette shook the paper out, opened it. Next to the by now familiar photograph of The Kiss, the headline read, TRUDI PATRIDES TO WED ALEX ST CLOUD. The lines blurred as she read them.

'"I tried to stay away from him", said sexy Trudi Patrides this morning, "but I couldn't. He's the most marvellous man in the world, and I love him to bits." Trudi, who is currently divorcing husband of six months Hal Patrides, middle-aged chairman of Tempest Air Design, is launching her film career this week with a starring role in *Deathwatch*, co-starring . . .'

'Isn't it good news, miss?' demanded Arnold. For once his smile had faded, and he peered at her with concerned blue eyes, his lips trembling.

'It's very good news, Arnie,' she said, but his old eyes were filling with tears in response to her own, and she dropped the paper and walked blindly back home, oblivious of Arnold or any of the other people who stopped to look at the tears on her cheeks.

Well, that question had been answered now. And answered in full. Before it had even occurred to her that there might be a fight for Alex St Cloud, the battle had been lost and won.

There was a familiar blue Jaguar parked on the edge of the Heath outside her garden, and as she walked up numbly, Mark Macmillan opened the door and got out. His handsome, vapid face was wearing an expression of concern.

'Nicky—sweetheart! You've been crying!'

'Don't you *dare* sweetheart me,' she snapped, wiping the tears off her cheeks with the back of her wrist. 'What do you want?'

'I've been trying to phone you all day,' he said uncomfortably. 'It seems everybody else in London had the same idea.' He kissed her gingerly on the cheek. 'I say, Nicky, let's go in. I'll make you a cup of tea if you like. Okay?'

'Okay,' she sniffled, suddenly pleased to have someone to talk to, even Mark Macmillan. She sat numbly while Mark busied himself in the kitchen, waiting for the pain to hit her. The hot tea was comforting, and she looked at Mark over her cup with wet-lashed eyes.

'What brings you here, Mark? I thought everything between us was over.'

He winced. 'Look, Nicky—'

'I hate being called Nicky,' she said suddenly.

'Do you?' he blinked. 'Why on earth didn't you ever tell me?'

She shrugged. 'I don't know. It never occurred to me.'

Mark sighed. 'We weren't really very well suited, were we, Nicky—Nicolette, I mean.'

'No, I suppose we weren't.' They looked at one another.

'Look,' said Mark, dropping his eyes, and fiddling with a button on his jacket, 'I've—I've treated you pretty meanly and shoddily. I—I'm sorry, Nicky—Nicolette.'

'It doesn't matter,' she sighed. 'It's all over with now.'

'Is it? Tell me, old thing—this Alex St Cloud. Does he mean a lot to you?'

She stared at him, trying to think of some way to tell him, trying to find some words to describe how she felt about the man she wanted to marry, whose children she wanted to have—

'Never mind,' he said quietly. 'I can see the answer in your face.' He sipped his tea, looking guilty. 'Odd thing,' he said, 'all that newspaper fuss—it was partly my fault, I'm afraid.'

'Yours? How?'

'Trudi Patrides,' he said succinctly.

Nicolette looked at him, beginning to work out the story in her mind.

'How do you know her?' she asked.

'She's very fashionable,' said Mark, as though that explained everything. 'I'd become quite friendly with her.' He met Nicolette's eyes, and then coloured guiltily. 'Well, she was rather leading me round on a string.'

'Geraldine—*and* Trudi?' she asked acidly.

'I'm not in a big enough league to keep Trudi Patrides satisfied for very long,' he said with a bitter inflection.

'But you told her about me and Alex?' He nodded again. 'And she told the papers?' He nodded again, sighing.

'It's all about *Deathwatch*,' he explained. 'This new film of hers. Apparently she's been cherishing this dream for years of becoming a film-star. She finally persuaded some fool to put up the money, and cast herself as the heroine in this ghastly thriller. It's been on the go for months.'

Nicolette listened, staring out of the window across the Heath to the blue sky beyond.

'She needed some publicity stunt to launch the damned thing,' Mark continued. 'She was thinking about staging a mock execution in Trafalgar Square.' He shuddered. 'That sort of thing. Anyway, the climax of *Deathwatch* concerns the hero and heroine being marooned on a yacht in the middle of the South Atlantic—'

She stared at Mark with unhappy brown eyes. He nodded. 'Yes. A close enough parallel to you and Alex on *Mistral* to be irresistible.'

'You mean—'

'She's got a hell of a lot of contacts among the press,' Mark sighed. 'Enough to make sure that *Mistral* stayed headline news for days. And to ensure that your arrival in Portsmouth would be the focus of every newspaper and television company in the country.'

'But why—?'

'Think of all that free publicity, Nicky. Nationwide, saturation coverage, totally free publicity for Trudi Reinhart and *Deathwatch*. It's going to mean millions to her in terms of box-office sales.'

She sat frozen in her chair. 'I've just read a report,' she said slowly, 'claiming that she and Alex are going to get married.'

Mark nodded. 'Also part of her publicity scheme, old girl. I don't know whether she actually intends to go through with the marriage or not. She'll probably drop the whole thing—and your Alex—once she feels she's got enough mileage out of it.' He drained his cup. 'Don't look so tragic, old girl—you'll get him back in the end.'

'Alex is in love with her,' she answered dully. 'That's how she's managed to blind him like this, Mark.'

'Oh,' said Mark. He looked at her with sympathetic eyes. 'It's all in rather a mess, isn't it?'

'It's been in a mess ever since Serengeti, Mark. Perhaps since even before then. God, I feel so miserable—'

'Steady on,' said Mark worriedly. 'This won't last, you know—Trudi's just jumped on your band-wagon, so to speak. Maybe—' He hesitated. 'Maybe he'll come back to you, once—'

'Once she's through with him? No,' she said, anger beginning to replace her pain, 'I'm not that much of a softie, Mark.'

'It wouldn't be soft, Nicky—'

'Oh yes, it would. I don't care for other women's leavings, Mark. I've got my pride. If Alex is back with Trudi whatever-her-name-is, then let him stay there!'

Liar, said her heart, liar.

Mark looked up. 'We could still always get married,' he said hopefully. 'Or at least give each other a try. What say? Let's go out somewhere to-night—like old times!'

'The times aren't that old,' she reminded him drily.

'Nicky—Nicolette—look, I've been a swine to you, I know that. And when you said I'd engineered that conversation—about Geraldine—well, you were right. I did. For some crazy reason I was desperate to leave you—'

'Trudi Patrides is not a crazy reason,' she retorted sourly.

He winced. 'It wasn't just that, Nicolette. I was so confused. I really didn't know what I wanted. After I got—'

'Got rid of me?' she suggested calmly. He winced again.

'After we said goodbye on the telephone, I thought I'd done the right thing. But now—'

'Now you're beginning to change your mind?'

'Well,' he said. 'You're different, somehow.' He glanced at her with flattering eyes. 'Your skin's gone such a lovely colour. And your hair—it really suits you that length. I don't know where you got it cut, but it's lovely.

And your figure—Nicky, you look like something out of a Hollywood heaven!'

'Very complimentary,' she said drily, then relented. 'Look, Mark—the tan will fade, the figure will go, sooner or later the hair will go grey. You can't base a relationship on what people look like. There has to be something more.'

'But there is,' he assured her earnestly. 'I've been getting myself straight lately, Nicky. I'm a reformed character—honestly!' He looked at her with pleading eyes. 'Let's give it a whirl—what do you say?'

She looked at him, comparing him mentally to Alex's power, Alex's surging energy, Alex's unflinching honesty of spirit.

'I don't think so, Mark,' she said gently. 'But thanks for the offer all the same.'

'Please, Nicky—let's just go riding together, across the downs, the way we used to—just once?'

'We'd better not,' she said, as kindly as she could.

Mark sighed, his face sad. 'I guess I deserve all this, Nicolette. I've been a complete fool, and I suppose I merit some kind of punishment—'

'I'm not trying to punish you, Mark,' she said patiently. 'I simply don't want to start anything new with you—or with anyone, for that matter.'

He glanced at her. 'You really love this Alex, don't you?'

'Don't ask me that again, Mark,' she said quietly. 'You know the answer.'

'I suppose it's natural,' he sighed. 'He sounds like quite a guy.' His slightly petulant mouth turned down bitterly at the corners. 'I got one or two lectures on him from

Trudi from time to time. He's the best at everything, it seems—'

'I don't want to know,' she said sharply, standing up.

Mark rose with her, buttoning his jacket.

'I'm sorry, Nicky. I wish I could do something to help you out. Maybe I could go to Alex and tell him—'

'Please—for God's sake—don't do anything so childish,' she said firmly. Her brown eyes stared out into the creamy sky beyond her privet-hedge absently. 'She'll break his heart, you know, Mark. Once he finds out that she's just using him to further her career—it'll break his heart.'

'Then why don't you tell him?' suggested Mark. 'Write to him, call him up—tell him about Trudi. Tell him what I've told you—'

'I told you, Mark, I've got my pride. I wouldn't go back to Alex if he came here on his knees.' She ushered him to the door. 'Let her break his heart. If he's stupid enough to let her. It won't cost me any sleepless nights.'

Liar, said her heart.

Liar.

But her anger stayed with her. She cultivated it, nurtured it. It was at least preferable to the miserable sense of loss that made her heart ache. She was angry even as she sat cleaning the cracked varnish off an eighteenth-century landscape, waiting for the telephone to ring, and to hear Alex's voice telling her it wasn't true.

And she was angrier still when he didn't ring. Motivated by some obscure jealousy, she went to see *Deathwatch* with a girl friend. Trudi Reinhart came over as a soulless

vamp, all shaking breasts and wet red lips. Or so she told
herself. She didn't stay more than half an hour, anyway.
At the first clinch in the film, when Trudi's vast screen lips
had clamped on to the hero's, with all the tenderness and
passion of space-craft colliding in a science fiction film,
she had got up and walked out, her heart aching with the
image of Alex in that woman's arms. Her friend had
followed resignedly, saying, 'You can't be brooding about
him for ever, Nicolette. You've got to forget him some
time.'

Two days turned into three, four, five. The little flicker
of hope in her slowly faded and died. Deep inside her there
had been a little voice that said, 'It's all a terrible mis-
take—he'll be back.' The voice grew softer, and died
away.

A commission took her up to Northumbria for three
days, staying in an old country house owned by a man
called Deverell, who had begun to suspect that the sombre
canvases on his walls might conceal lost masterpieces. She
spent hours with the grisly collection, cleaning off two
centuries and more of encrusted dirt and tacky brown
varnish, to reveal an undistinguished collection of lop-
sided dogs and dead pheasants on carpets, unbelievably
ugly ancestors, solemn children, bowls of inedible-looking
fruit.

Mr Deverell sighed as he wrote out her cheque.

'I rather preferred them the way they were,' he said,
averting his gaze from the steely eyes of a vitriolic-looking
great-great-grandmother. Nicolette went back to London.

The news that she was no longer engaged to Mark
Macmillan and separated from Alex St Cloud had
brought a trickle of tentative telephone calls from ex-boy-

friends and hopeful boy-friends-to-be. She was slightly disturbed to discover that unsuspected passions had lurked in the breasts of several of her male acquaintances for months. She steadfastly refused all their invitations, until one of them, echoing her girl friend of a week earlier, warned her, 'You'd better start forgetting him, Nicky. Have some fun—get out and meet some new people. Shake his dust off your feet.' The next offer, she decided, she would accept.

It was from a handsome Chinese boy called Paul Chong, who was charming, urbane, amusing, sexy and— not Alex St Cloud.

In the meantime, she kept a dull eye on the papers, watching for news of Alex and Trudi. Had she been able to admit it to herself, she was waiting for news that their engagement had been broken off. There was no such news.

A boy from the British Museum took her out to an expensive French restaurant, ran out of petrol on the way back, and kissed her expertly until she swung herself out of the car, revolted, and took a passing taxi home.

More commissions came in. Nicolette read them over breakfast, picked up her teapot, and threw it across the room with sudden fury and hurt.

'Damn you, Alex!' she whispered. Then she fetched a broom to sweep up the pieces, muttering angrily. It had been a favourite teapot.

In Manchester, a deranged art student walked into a big art gallery and hacked a hole in a large and hideous modern painting. The director of the gallery, in his private capacity, rather approved of the student's critical tastes. In his public capacity, he telephoned Nicolette.

'Yes,' she told him wearily, 'I think I can do it, Mr

Rogers. Yes, I'll be up on—er—shall we say Thursday? It's a pleasure. Yes—thank you. Goodbye.'

She stood by the telephone, running her hand through her fair hair, which was at last growing into its usual flowing curls. Something thudded heavily into her wrist as she lowered her arm. It was a heavy silver bracelet, found in a ruined Moorish castle on an island in the Red Sea. As she stared at it, lost in a warm, hazy memory, the telephone rang again. She picked it up. It was Alex.

CHAPTER NINE

'NICOLETTE?'

'H-Hullo, Alex,' she said, her throat suddenly dry. She sat down abruptly—her knees had turned to jelly.

'I'm sorry I haven't called you for so long, but—'

'Oh, I quite understand,' she said bitterly. 'You've had other fish to fry, haven't you?'

'You sound like the heroine in some domestic drama,' he commented, his deep voice amused.

'Do I?' she said icily. 'You should know, Alex—you must be an expert on domestic dramas by now.'

He snorted. 'Nicolette, you and I are going out to-night.'

'Oh, are we indeed?' she exclaimed angrily, her temper rising at his cool arrogance. 'Well, you can just think again, Alex! I happen to be extremely busy.'

'Not too busy for what I have in mind.'

'You've got a damn nerve, Alex!' she began furiously, 'You just dropped me like a hot potato, I don't hear from you for *weeks*—'

'One week,' he interrupted, the smile still in his voice.

'—and then you've got the *gall* to ring me up and order me around! Who on earth do you think you are?'

'Come off your high horse, Nicolette,' he retorted.

'And why the sudden interest in poor little Nicolette Mercury all of a sudden?' she pursued nastily. 'Has Trudi finished with you?'

There was a tense little silence.

'Look, Nicolette,' Alex said patiently, 'I know you've been hurt and upset, but—'

'Hurt? Not by you, Alex,' she snapped. 'You flatter yourself to think that anything *you* could do could hurt me!'

'I didn't expect you to be so angry, Nicolette,' he said quietly.

'Then you don't know much about women, Alex,' she retorted. 'Not as much as you like to think you know, anyway. Although maybe,' she added viciously, 'women have changed since the days when *you* were young!'

'Nicolette!'

'Go back to Trudi Reinhart, Alex. Or is she still calling herself Patrides?'

'I don't know what she's calling herself,' he said, his own anger beginning to rise now, 'and I don't care. Nicolette—'

'You're too old for me, Alex,' she said cruelly. 'You said so yourself, didn't you? Too old and hard and cynical. Although I admit my estimation of your hardness has gone down since last time I saw you—kissing Trudi Bloody Reinhart in front of twenty million viewers!'

'There were several times during that voyage, Nicolette, when I almost put you over my knee.' He took a deep breath. 'I'm beginning to be sorry I didn't. But I promise you this, young lady—if you ever speak to me like that again, I shall make you regret it extremely bitterly!'

Nicolette cleared her throat. Her nasty remarks suddenly didn't seem so clever after all.

'Leave me alone, Alex. I'm not interested in you,' she said quietly.

'But I'm interested in you, Nicolette,' he said firmly.

'Are you? Well, I don't want what Trudi Reinhart has chewed over and spat out, Alex—'

'Nicolette,' he said, his voice cutting through her sentence like an Arctic wind through thin muslin, 'I'm coming to pick you up at six-thirty to-night. At your place. Understood?'

'Don't try to bully me, Alex,' she said, trying to sound as brave as she wanted to. 'I'm not—'

'At six-thirty, Nicolette,' he said icily.

'And if I choose not to be available?'

'Then I'll come looking for you,' he said succinctly. 'And by the way, dress is formal.'

'I'm not going to be here, Alex,' she snapped, 'I'm—' The line purred in her ear, and she slammed the phone down furiously. 'I wish I hadn't broken that teapot now,' she muttered to the telephone. 'I feel in need of something to throw!' She stormed through her front door, through her tiny garden, and on to the Heath. Arrogant pig! If he thought she was going to come running at his whistle, then he was very, very wrong. She strode furiously across the Heath. What did he think she was? The bangle clunked against her wrist, and she stared down at it, a thick silver hoop encircling her slender wrist. With a sudden spasm of rage she snatched it off and hurled it as far as she could into a nearby thicket. Immediately, she regretted her action, her heart twisting painfully as the glittering thing descended with a crash into the undergrowth. Biting her lip, she turned on her heel and walked off, telling herself that she was glad, glad, glad, and wondering where she could hide to-night to get away from Alex St Cloud.

Arnold the paper-boy was standing at one end of the Heath, clutching his armful of papers, and staring vacantly at the tall houses opposite. He turned as she came, and his faded blue eyes lit up.

'I been waiting for you, miss,' he exclaimed.

'Have you, Arnie? Why?'

'I'm really sorry about that paper, miss,' he said earnestly, his lined face concerned. 'I didn't know as it would make you cry. I'm real sorry, miss—honest!'

'Oh, Arnie,' she sighed, looking remorsefully at the worried old face. 'I didn't mean to upset you with my stupid crying. I was just overtired that night.'

'Tired?' His eyes sparkled again. 'You been to Africa, miss!'

'That's right, Arnie,' she smiled. An elderly couple stopped to buy the morning paper, and Arnold dealt them their change coin by coin. 'You seen the tigers, miss?' he asked eagerly.

'Oh yes,' she nodded. 'Stripey, they were, with green eyes and teeth like this.' She drew vast pegs in the air with her forefinger. Arnold was suitably impressed.

As she walked slowly across the Heath towards her little house, she felt calmer. No, she decided, she was *not* going anywhere with Alex St Cloud, tonight or any other time. She was just beginning to get over him, wasn't she? She would simply not be in to-night when Alex came.

Then she remembered that Josephine Littlefield was coming round for tea that afternoon. Jo was a good friend—she would spend the night at her house. Pleased she had remembered about Jo's visit, she cut across the Heath to Mabon's Cake Shop, and bought some jam tarts.

Jo arrived at three o'clock, a small, untidy person with an abundance of curly brown hair and mole-like, clever little eyes. Nicolette had always been fond of her, and their friendship extended back to schooldays.

She told Jo the story on her striped settee, and her friend watched her with shiny brown eyes that seemed to understand a great deal more than they let on. When Nicolette had finished, Jo picked up a jam tart and nibbled at it thoughtfully.

'So—what are you going to do?' she asked.

'I was hoping you'd let me spend the night at your flat, Jo. I just don't want to be in when he comes.'

Jo blinked. 'Why ever not? You love him, don't you?' The directness of the question took her breath away, and Nicolette blinked in her turn.

'No, I don't,' she said.

'Oh yes, you do,' said Jo calmly, polishing off the jam tart with relish. 'You didn't love Mark Macmillan, Nicolette—I always knew that. With this man it's different. I can see it in your face, in your looks, in everything you do. Go and buy something nice to wear this afternoon—I'll come and help you choose a dress.'

'What? And take him back, after he's been consorting with that—that *creature*?'

'It's not a question of taking him back,' said Jo reasonably, tucking into her second jam tart. 'You never had him in the first place, did you?'

Nicolette paused.

'I mean, he was never actually your lover, was he? And if he had some unfinished business with this Trudi Reinhart then that's got nothing to do with you.'

'But—'

'Where did you chuck that bangle he gave you?'

'Over there,' said Nicolette, gesturing at the thicket, which was visible over her untidy privet hedge. Jo squinted at the clump of shrubbery with wise little eyes.

'It looks thorny. Have you got a couple of pairs of gardening gloves?'

'Josephine,' said Nicolette sharply, 'I am not going to go looking for that bangle. And I am *not* going anywhere with Alex St Cloud to-night. The very thought of sitting in the same car with him—' She stopped.

'What?' asked Jo. 'Thrills you? Excites you? Let's go and find that bracelet, Nicolette. And then let's go and spend some of your hard-earned money on something long and slinky and sexy.'

'You aren't listening, Jo,' said Nicolette angrily. 'I hate Alex! I don't ever want to see him again!'

'Do you mean that?' asked Jo gently.

'Of course I do,' she snapped.

'Then tell him so.'

'*What?*'

Jo smiled, picking up the last jam tart. 'I said, tell him so. Face to face. Have some pride, Nicolette, for God's sake—you can't just cower away while this man comes to see you—that's the coward's way out.'

'But—' she gasped.

'There are no buts to it. Are you a woman or a mouse?'

'Jo, I—'

'You can't duck out of this, Nicolette.' Jo's bright button eyes were unexpectedly firm. 'If you just slink off and hide, you'll never know *what* you feel about him. Believe me. Why, I've never heard such an exciting story—you meet him wandering alone among the lions and elephants, cut off all your hair to get on his boat, go through a hurricane together—and now you want to slope off and hide when he comes to take you out!'

Nicolette stared at her friend blankly.

'Listen to me, Nicolette—if you want to forget Alex St Cloud, then you've got to see him one last time. Dressed to the nines. Show him what you're made of, girl! Dazzle him, stand up to him—and *then* walk out on him. If you want to.'

'But—but—Jo, I don't trust—'

'Don't trust who?' asked her friend as she paused helplessly. 'You don't trust yourself, isn't that it?'

'You're confusing me, Jo.'

'You're confusing *me*,' retorted Jo, brushing jammy crumbs off her plump lips. 'Is this the same Nicolette Mercury who climbed the apple-tree with me to get our kite back? And who punched the school bully's nose?' Josephine rose to her full height of four feet eleven, and pulled her rumpled frock straight. 'Let's go and find that bangle!'

At six-fifteen, Nicolette was still sitting in front of her mirror, staring at her own golden-tanned face. Despite all her resolutions, a deep thrill of excitement was running through her, as though a swarm of icy little fishes were swimming around in her blood. She had chosen the most dazzling—and the most expensive—gown in the boutique eventually. She glanced at the shimmering violet silk across her golden shoulders. Was it *too* décolleté? The sweeping vee of the neckline emphasised, rather than concealed, the splendid curve of her bust. She had never in her life dreamed of wearing a garment like this one. But as

Jo had remarked, when you're going to make his tongue hang out, you might as well go the whole hog. The gown was a pale, pearly violet, a colour deep enough to pick up the mauve hints in the white mink she was going to wear. The little diamond pendant that was her father's last gift sent out a starry blaze against her tanned skin, and the sapphire studs in her earlobes glittered coldly, the way stars do in an African night. She had brushed her hair till it gleamed like burnished metal, and had let it fall like two golden gull's wings against her cheeks. As for her face— she knew that if ever in her life she was going to look truly beautiful, then it was to-night.

Without vanity, she looked at herself. The days on *Mistral* had gilded her skin, brought a hint of dusky roses to her cheeks. She had not needed more than a touch of red gloss on her lips and a dusting of eye-shadow to bring out the summer colours in her face. Her brown eyes, always such a startling contrast to her blonde hair, glowed like some rare and precious stones. She rose, her heart beating faster, and slipped the fine white glove over her hand, deciding to carry the other one. In the mirror, she was radiant—a slender goddess of summer, with a touch of voluptuous ripeness at her bust, a full, deep beauty in her face. She was going to make Alex regret ever having left her tonight!

She glanced at the clock. Almost six-thirty. It would not be like Alex to be late, she knew. Perhaps she had better lock up, and go and wait downstairs—

The distant chopping roar had grown steadily louder, and as the tall cypress in her garden swayed in some quick breeze, she turned to stare out over Hampstead Heath. And gasped.

The scarlet helicopter was hovering down on to the Heath with the grace of a jewelled dragonfly settling on a lily-pad. The wind from its whirling rotors was sweeping the rough grass flat in a wide circle around it, and the beat of its engines was resounding across the rolling hillocks of the Heath.

The helicopter landed gently, and then its whirling blades slowed steadily as the snarl of the engine died down. The door in the canopy opened, and a man in an evening suit stepped out and began to walk towards her house. *Alex*. Before she could stop it, a smile of pure joy rose to her lips. Alex! Only Alex would think of arriving in a helicopter! Laughing, Nicolette ran downstairs to meet him, then paused, checked herself in the little hallway, and greeted him with cool eyes as she opened the door.

'Hullo, Nicolette,' he purred. She gaped. He was— magnificent! She had become so used to seeing him in shorts, with his splendid torso naked and tanned, that to see him now, looking so incredibly urbane and sophisticated, was a shock. The slate-grey eyes met hers, jolting her heart, then dropped to take in her gown. 'You're more beautiful even than I remembered,' he said, the ironic curve of his mouth mocking her.

'Good evening, Mr St Cloud,' she said coolly, offering him her hand—the gloved one. He was supremely elegant in the severity of black and white, wearing a suit that fitted his athlete's body like a glove. Strange that he should be even sexier and more desirable dressed to the hilt than when nearly naked and gleaming with sweat. He took her arm gently and waved at the helicopter.

'Shall we go? So,' he smiled, as they walked through her little garden, 'it's to be Mr St Cloud, is it? Then I had better call you Miss Mercury.' The thrilling, smoky eyes caressed her, and she looked away, wondering how long she was going to be able to play this game.

The burghers of Hampstead Heath had gathered in their doorways to stare in astonishment as this phenomenon in their midst. Alex walked her to the gleaming machine as though it were the most natural thing in the world, oblivious to the gaping faces, the clusters of children marvelling in the front gardens.

'May I help you up, Miss Mercury?' A strong brown hand lifted her into the black-padded interior of the machine. How could anyone, she wondered, help a woman into a helicopter with the innate grace of an earl helping a duchess into a coach-and-six? The bucket seat was beautifully comfortable, and as Alex buckled the seat-belt around her slender waist, he said conversationally, 'Doesn't this remind you of the safety harnesses on board *Mistral*?'

'No,' she said firmly, 'it does not.' She watched him, trying to conceal her apprehension as he climbed into the pilot's seat and began checking the controls.

'Ever flown in one of these before?' he asked with a grin.

'No,' she said. 'They've always seemed very noisy, dangerous things to me.'

'This one isn't,' he said, unperturbed. He pressed the ignition, and the rotors began spinning with the familiar chopping roar. Alex slammed the Perspex canopy door shut, and the sound was instantly excluded.

'Pick a tape,' he invited, and she leaned forward, trying not to show how impressed she was, to select a cassette from the rack on the console. She pushed the tape into the neat recorder, and the civilised strains of a Mozart piano concerto filled the little cockpit. She glanced out of the window. The late afternoon had sent long shadows running across the sunlit grass. The peace of full summer was on the world, and she looked up into the cloudless blue sky overhead. How odd to think that soon she was going to be up there, drifting through the air like a bird—

With a gracious wave to Nicolette's neighbours, Alex pulled back the throttle, and with a slight lurch, the peaceful landscape began to slip away beneath her. Suddenly alarmed, she clutched her seat tightly.

'Alex—' she gasped, 'I'm not sure I'm going to like this!'

'I thought I was Mr St Cloud,' he mocked gently. 'And I'm sure you're going to love it.'

Her stomach dropped with a hollow thrill as the machine rose slowly, then faster, leaving the bright Heath in the distance below them. Nicolette peered nervously out of the window at the receding houses, watching them dwindle into sheds, doll's houses, little red-topped boxes . . .

Hampstead Heath lay stretched below her, a brilliant gold-and-green handkerchief surrounded by a toyland of streets and houses. The sensation was as terrifying as the worst of the fairground machines she remembered from her girlhood. The scarlet helicopter lifted its dragonfly tail slightly, and then they were gliding swiftly forward, towards the heart of London.

Nicolette's heart was in her throat as she clutched the nylon webbing that secured her to her seat. Alex smiled quietly. 'Look,' he said. She looked forward, and her fear suddenly drained away from her. All London lay at her feet, a wonderful fairy city in the golden afternoon sunlight. As they swooped towards the centre of the city, she saw the Thames doubling its way through the maze of the city, a wide ribbon of blue glass that extended into the bright, hazy horizon, to the open sea beyond. And London, the greatest city of them all, spread out beneath her, a panorama of history gliding steadily past. It was like a dream, some intense childhood dream of wings, that had transported her beyond the bounds of everyday experience.

Alex tilted the controls, and the helicopter banked slightly, so that the city unfolded to Nicolette's left, crisp and clear in the warm sunlight. She watched their own shadow dizzily, a little ghost that flitted swiftly across the sunlit faces of wide streets full of traffic, green parks, tall granite buildings. She glanced at Alex. He was smiling quietly to himself. His hands on the controls were sure and strong, controlling the machine with expert strength. She marvelled at him, a devastatingly handsome figure in a beautiful suit, towering above the city in this minor miracle of technology.

'I told you you would love it,' he reminded her.

'It's wonderful,' she breathed. 'It's like a dream—' She bit her lip, determined not to respond to him any more.

'There's Hyde Park.'

The trees that flew beneath them were like the models in a child's railway set, the canal a glittering snail's trail through the greenery. Above them, the great dome of the sky was bright and almost cloudless. Away to the east, the young moon had appeared milkily over the horizon, and a few faint stars were already visible in the soft blue depths above.

'I'm surprised Trudi let you out to-night,' she said

acidly, trying to break the spell that all this beauty was casting over her. Alex merely grinned.

Trafalgar Square drifted beneath them, dominated by the immense, grey-roofed Gallery and the towering column in the centre. The roofs of the city were unexpectedly beautiful, an abstract arrangement of pinks and fawns and greys, crenellated, tiled, balconied, sometimes containing unexpected gardens and once or twice the turquoise square of a swimming-pool.

They passed the grey grandeur of the Houses of Parliament, and again the helicopter banked under Alex's touch. They raced diagonally across the river, gaining a privileged vision of its great bridges that succeeded one another westward to Richmond and eastward to Woolwich and the sea beyond. The ships on the water were dark against its steely glitter, and Nicolette watched their own shadow flit across the surface of the river. How many faces, she wondered, would be turning up to glance at the red dragonfly that darted over them? Would this vast city, so accustomed to excitement and novelty, be sparing them even a cursory glance?

'Do you like my toy?' Alex asked with an amused glitter in his eyes.

'It's a toy for very rich and spoiled little boys,' she commented, trying to take the wind out of his sails.

'Not at all,' he corrected her smoothly. 'You could have one for a lot less than the cost of a Rolls-Royce.'

'Is it one of your designs?' she asked.

He nodded, his eyes bright with pride. 'Every nut and bolt of her.'

Nicolette stared out at the panoramic vision around them.

'I'm beginning to understand your preference for air over water,' she remarked. 'I've never seen anything as lovely as this, Alex.'

'You deserved a treat,' he said obliquely, 'For being so patient.'

'While you dallied with that—that sex-queen?' she retorted. 'I hope you don't think that—'

'Hush,' he smiled. 'Let's leave all that till much later, little virgin. There are many things about the world that you have yet to understand.'

Nicolette snorted, but did not comment.

The trees and green grass of Greenwich drifted up and under them, and then were gone. Now they were racing south, the suburbs below unfolding in rapid succession, alternating with factories, the thin bright ribbons of railway lines, the red streets populated by little coloured car-roofs, the tiny gardens with their tiny, neat flower-beds. It was all so very neat, so ordered, so tidy. It was hard to believe that real people lived and quarrelled down there, a vast multitude of ants, each with their own distinct ant-identities!

The sprawling suburbs began to give way to larger and longer stretches of green, allotments, fields, open country. Nicolette turned anxiously to Alex.

'Where are we going?' she demanded.

'Chez Maxim,' he smiled, his grey eyes meeting hers with a hint of their old challenge. She blinked.

'Maxim's? In *Paris*?'

'Certainly,' he said urbanely, and glanced at his watch. 'I've booked a table for eight—we should be in excellent time.'

'*Alex!*'

'We're coming over Croydon, by the way,' he purred. 'Are you enjoying the flight?'

She stared at him, astounded by his calm.

'B-but—*Paris!* Alex, I don't even have any passport!'

'I don't think anyone is going to ask you for it at Maxim's,' he said drily.

'This must be costing you an absolute *fortune*,' she said in bewilderment. 'Couldn't you just have taken me to the local fish and chip shop?'

'There'll be plenty of time for economies later,' he said calmly. 'After the marriage.'

'After whose marriage?' she snapped, tugging her mink closer around her. Ignoring her, Alex glanced up at the control panel above his head.

'I'm going to increase our speed slightly,' he said. 'Tunbridge Wells coming up fairly shortly. Want to see it?'

Kent unfolded beneath them, an endless counterpane of green, brown and yellow fields that rushed underneath them, studded with tiny houses, miniature cows and horses, tiny winding streams that sparkled in the late afternoon sun. Nicolette sat back in her seat, breathless. She had meant to be so calm, so cool, so chilling to Alex! How on earth could she have expected *this*!

He was quiet, obviously intent on flying the helicopter, and she simply relaxed and stared dreamily out of the big Perspex bubble at England unrolling beneath them. Whatever happened to her to-night, whatever became of her and Alex, she knew she was never going to forget this. Never going to forget Alex St Cloud. The little fields drifted swiftly past, and as the milky blue deepened into the ultramarine of a summer evening, the stars came out one by one around them.

And then they had flashed over the chalk cliffs between Hastings and Dungeness, and the Channel was below them, a choppy grey sheet, covered with the tiny white wrinkles of waves.

'Has *Mistral* been repaired?' she asked him, lolling her head sideways on the padded seat. Alex nodded.

'Olafsen bought her in the end. The Trans-Atlantic Yacht Race starts in a month's time, and there's every chance that Olafsen's going to win it in *Mistral*. That'll be a big boost for my father.'

'Did you ever get any damages from Julian?'

'I didn't even bother,' he said calmly. A fishing trawler drifted beneath them, close enough for Nicolette to see the figures waving on its decks. Alex indicated the long dark line on the horizon.

'France,' he said succinctly.

'We must be going like the wind,' she said, astonished.

Alex nodded. 'Helicopters can be very deceptive. We're going at the same speed as any light aircraft. And we're taking a much directer route.' He checked his watch. 'We're going to be early, I'm afraid. Still, I don't think Pierre will mind. Do you?' He glanced at her with mocking grey eyes, the dying sun gilding his beautiful face. 'It's a long way to go for dinner,' he admitted, 'but we have to admit that the English have their limitations. One of them,' he grinned, 'is cooking!'

The red helicopter drifted out of the purple dusk over the streets of Paris and settled like a brilliant butterfly high on the roof of the Chrysler Centre. As Alex settled the machine neatly in the bull's eye of the circular landing-pad, Nicolette blinked to make sure she was not dreaming. The distant fretwork of the Eiffel Tower swooped up into the evening sky beyond. High above the streets, the unmistakable smell of Paris reached them, compounded of chocolate and gasoline and a million herbs and spices. As the uniformed commissionaire helped her with a beaming smile out of the canopy, she was feeling distinctly dizzy. The suddenness of it all, the magical speed with which events had unfolded, had left her slightly breathless. Alex took her arm firmly, as though understanding.

'You'll be able to settle down to the best cocktails in Paris in a few minutes,' he smiled.

The head waiter who came bowing up to them in the discreetly-lit foyer of the famous restaurant greeted Alex like an old friend, conversing in French too fast for Nicolette to follow. Almost overawed by the elegance of her surroundings (there was a real Utrillo hanging on the silk-papered wall), she clung to Alex's arm as they walked through the plush velvet curtains and descended the stairs to the restaurant. And were greeted by a cascade of roses—an arrangement of literally thousands of blooms, a scented crimson waterfall that dripped from the white marble urn. The four-piece band beyond were playing sweet jazz blues to the dozens of diners in the magnificently-appointed room.

'Alex,' she whispered, 'it's wonderful!'

'Yes,' he smiled. 'But we're going to be a little more private to-night—*n'est-ce pas, Pierre?*'

'*Oui, M'sieur St Cloud*. The *salon* is ready.'

The waiter ushered them into the big oak doorway. The long room was dominated by the most stupendous chandelier Nicolette had ever seen, a frozen, inverted fountain of dazzling crystal which glittered frostily in the candlelight, glowing with unearthly splendour. At the far end of the room, next to a positive bank of lilies and roses, an oval dining-table had been laid for two, silver and crystal glinting on the damask. The remainder of the room had been set out as an eighteenth-century *salon*, with a beautiful Louis XVI chaise-longue, velvet drapes, another cascade of roses twining down a marble pillar—and a big, old-fashioned bow-window, covered with thick brocade curtains.

Alex turned to the waiter.

'I think we'll have the curtains open, Pierre.'

'Mais certainement, M'sieur St Cloud.'

He pulled the heavy drapes back, and belted them to the brass hook on the wall. Paris lay spread out beyond the gracefully leaded panes—a sparkling, twilight city, coming to bustling life as the sun set in glory in the west. Wordlessly, she walked with Alex to the window, and stared out over the fabulous view. The Arc de Triomphe and its radiating lines of traffic glowed in the beams of a thousand spotlights below. Nicolette turned to Alex with shining eyes.

'Alex—you mean it, don't you?'

'Mean what?' he smiled, his splendid face looking down at her with tender eyes.

'Me,' she said simply. 'And you.'

'Yes,' he said gently, 'I mean it.'

Their eyes met, explored each other, smiled deeply. Her stomach jolted in that sudden, electric shock, and Alex's eyes dropped to her mouth. The waiter was discreetly arranging flowers on the marble column, and Alex turned to him.

'We'll just have a drink to begin with, Pierre—I think Madame wants to relax a little before we eat.'

'Of course,' bowed the waiter.

'I'll have a whisky—my usual blend—and I think a *crème de menthe frappé* for Madame.'

'I'm Mademoiselle,' she said huskily when the waiter had gone. Alex's smile was beautiful.

'Not for much longer,' he told her calmly.

'Alex—' she whispered. Then she was in his arms, feeling the glorious hardness of his body through the thin silk of her gown, feeling his arms crushing her to him, all the ache and loneliness and misery leaving her in one voluptuous shudder. She raised her mouth to his, her lips clinging to his tenderly, with a loving eroticism that made him answer her trembling, then they sank into a kiss as endless and as gentle as the warm seas through which they had travelled so far to reach this exquisite moment, high above the streets of Paris. Down they drifted, down, down, into a tender passion that engulfed them, swept away every other thought, ran through their bodies and minds like fire. When at last they parted, she was dewy-eyed and weak. The light in his eyes was dazzling.

'My dear . . .' he whispered, drawing his finger softly down the side of her cheek, down her silky neck, across her smooth golden shoulder. She sighed, her skin shivering under his touch, and let her cheek rest against his palm, her long lashes fluttering closed over his eyes.

'Come and sit down,' he said, his voice deep and husky. Then he paused with a smile. 'Look, Pierre has brought our drinks—and we never even noticed!'

'Pierre is a jewel of discretion,' she murmured as they sat down on the chaise-longue. She looked down at her own slender hands resting so trustingly in Alex's palms. He closed elegant brown fingers over them and met her eyes with a smile that brought her skin up in goose-flesh.

'Alex, before I die—tell me where you've been these past ten days, for God's sake!'

'In Germany. As soon as I arrived, my chief negotiator was waiting for me with the contracts. I didn't even have time to shave properly before I was in one of our helicopters, bound for Bonn.'

'They've bought your design, haven't they?' she said, joy rising in her heart.

He nodded.

'Yes. They want twice as many as we at first estimated, too. And they might buy some of my light spotter aircraft as well—if I can sell them a package.'

'Oh, Alex!'

'*Oh, Alex* indeed,' he grinned. 'It looks as though we're going to be quite rich, Nicolette.'

'If we never have more than a pound to our names,' she told him gently, 'I'll still be the richest woman in the world.'

'You'll find I thrive on pretty compliments,' he said happily. His beautiful eyes dropped to her breast. 'It's a strange thing, my dear, but you're even sexier now—dressed like a goddess—than you were when I yanked your bikini off that night in the Red Sea.'

'I'm past blushing,' she smiled. 'But I was thinking the same thing about you earlier on.'

'You were?' This time the kiss was deliberately, deliciously sexy, an intimate caress that made her gasp and clutch at his shoulders.

'Wait,' she panted. 'Tell me about that *awful* woman—'

'Trudi?' He smiled. 'She's not so awful, really. She's just an opportunist.'

'She's a—' Nicolette paused, lost for a word which would combine decency with the depth of her feelings. 'When I read that she was going to marry you, I thought I was going to die,' she said, looking at him fiercely. 'I could have killed myself, Alex!'

'I don't think so,' he said with a hint of his old dryness. 'Anyway, at the time that announcement was being released to the press, Nicolette, I was explaining the finer points of rotor mechanics to a group of sixty very serious German engineers in Heidelberg.'

'But why didn't you deny it? Sue her?'

'What a waste of energy that would have been! It was beneath me to issue any statements about the affair at all. Besides, I didn't find out until a week later, when I got back to England.'

'I was so sure it was true!'

'And when did you stop being sure?'

'When Pierre pulled those curtains open,' she smiled. 'It came to me in a flash.'

'Like your idea for sneaking on to my yacht as Tommy Watson?'

'Wasn't it Timmy?'

'No, I'm sure it was Tommy.' They grinned at one another.

'I wonder if Bjorn Olafsen will ever know what went on aboard his yacht?' she mused.

'He's renamed it *Liv III*,' Alex told her.

'Very Swedish.'

Alex nodded, his eyes full of a grey light. 'My father's

building us another *Mistral*, Nicolette. For our wedding present.'

Her heart leaped inside her, and her joy threatened to spill out of her eyes. She looked hastily away, laying her hand on his silk shirt-front and tugging at the pearl button.

'I'm looking forward to meeting him,' she said huskily.

'We'll go down to Plymouth to-morrow. He's been dying to see you—ever since I told him we were getting married.'

'And when was that?'

'On the day we got back,' he grinned.

'*Alex*! Why didn't you bother to tell *me*?'

'Well, it sounded so unlikely at first. I had no idea myself until the words came out of my mouth. And then there was so much to do—people to meet, contracts to sign, pound notes to count—'

'I nearly stabbed you when you flung your arms around that Trudi—'

'I didn't fling my arms around her at all—she flung her arms around *me*!'

'You certainly looked as though you were enjoying it,' Nicolette said waspishly. He shrugged with a wicked smile.

'I was taken by surprise, that's all. In the heat of the moment, I may have seemed to be co-operating—'

'Seemed?'

'It was practically public assault,' he said reasonably. 'I was taken aback.'

'Nothing else?' she asked quietly.

His grey eyes met hers with a clear, loving light in them.

'Nothing else, Nicolette. It was all gone—all of it. You'd

swept it out of my heart, my darling—all the confusion, all the bitterness, all the pain—it had vanished like magic, and I didn't even know it.'

'Alex—'

'Trudi Reinhart means nothing to me, Nicolette. She never did mean anything. I was a fool—too big a fool even to know my own heart. I was fighting you all the way from Serengeti, Nicolette—fighting the love that was growing in me, fighting the desire for you that was making me burn—'

'And I was so frightened by you—frightened and fascinated! I fell in love with you that afternoon in Serengeti, you know. It just took *Mistral* to bring it home to me, Alex.'

'Huh—you fought like a wildcat!'

'Naturally—all you wanted was some quick sex.'

'Slow sex would have done as well,' he said with a glint in his eyes that made her look down at her hands demurely. 'But I understand your reservations, my darling—I guess I was pretty fierce at times.'

'Fierce? You made Captain Blood look like a Sunday School teacher! But my natural goodness saved me from a fate far worse than death.' She looked at him with solemn brown eyes, and he chuckled delightedly.

'I hope you haven't got any silly ideas about sex before marriage,' he said, looking at her cryptically over the rim of his glass.

'Which are the silly ideas,' she asked cautiously, 'the ones that approve of it? Or the ones that don't?'

Alex pretended shock. 'You mean you don't *know*? Nicolette!'

'All I know,' she said softly, reaching for his hands, 'is

that I love you, Alex. I love you so very much that it hurts.'

'Nicolette—' his voice was rough, his eyes like amethyst fire, 'you're all the world to me—and more. I love you, my darling, more than I'll ever be able to tell you.' He took her in his arms, and she melted against him, a flower of summer ready to burst into blossom. After the kiss, he took her hand shakily, and touched the silver bracelet at her wrist.

'I have a friend here in Paris who's a silversmith. He's making us a lock for this.'

'I'll never take it off anyway.'

'I trust you,' he smiled. 'I'll even give you the key. On Wednesdays and Sundays.'

'Why Wednesdays and Sundays?'

'Those are my days off.'

'Days off? I thought you were the boss!'

'You have to show an example. Oh, by the way—we're getting married next week.'

'Next week? I hate long engagements!'

'Listen, my dearest one, the chef will be in tears by now. We'd better eat.'

'*Enchantée, m'sieur.*'

'*Après vous, madame.*'

'By the way, darling,' said Nicolette with a sparkle in her eyes, 'you still owe me my wages.'

'What wages?' he asked in surprise, coming to take her in his arms.

'You promised to pay me the flat union rate—remember? Able Seaman Watson?'

'Oh, that.' Alex grinned. 'I'll give you your wages in kind. How's that?'

'In kind?' she protested. 'What kind do you have in mind, exactly, Mr St Cloud?'

'This kind,' he said gently. When he had finished kissing her, she was trembling again.

'You bosses are all the same,' she whispered, gazing up at him with adoring eyes, 'you just trample on the faces of the poor—'

He silenced her protests with his lips.

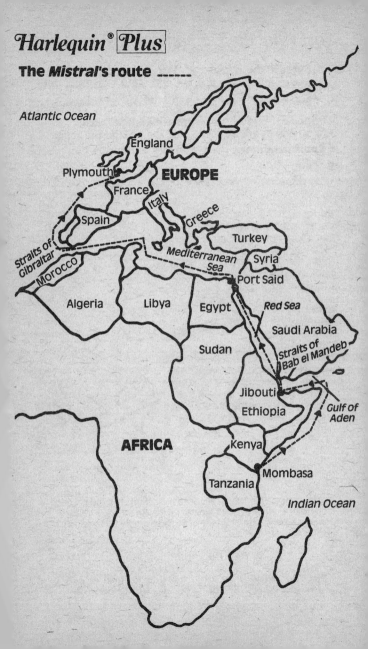

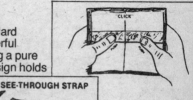
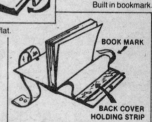